2—

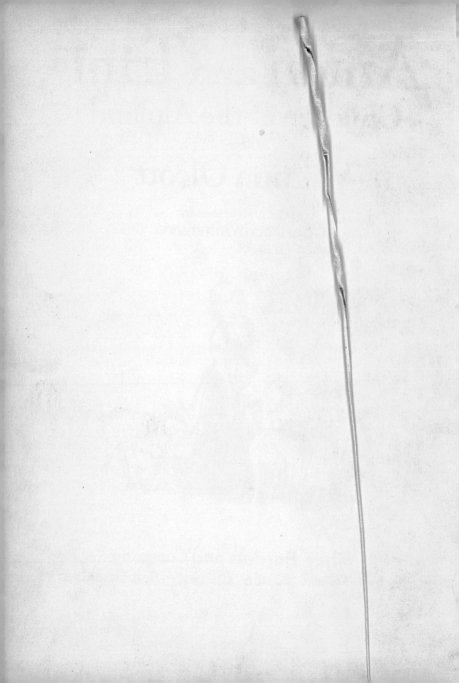

Anton and Trini
Children of the Alpland
by
Virginia Olcott

with illustrations by
Constance Whittemore

Silver, Burdett and Company
New York Newark Boston Chicago San Francisco

PRINTED IN THE UNITED STATES OF AMERICA

TO MY AUNTS
MARY WHITE OLCOTT
FRANCES OLCOTT

FOREWORD

Dear Boys and Girls:

A short while ago, when I was in Switzerland, I visited quaint old Swiss cities, peaceful towns, and quiet villages far up among the mountains. I saw modern factories and shops, up-to-date schools, and the comfortable homes of the Swiss people.

I was "a foreigner," but I did not feel strange, for the people of Switzerland think and dress much as we do in America. Indeed, just within the last few years, the peoples of Europe and America have been growing more and more alike. So I said to myself, "The ways of the Swiss are akin to our ways. Their men and women are interested in the things that interest us. Their children work and play and study as we do in our homes and schools. After all, things common to mankind are very much alike on both sides of the Atlantic. When I return home," said I, "I shall tell our boys and girls about the boys and girls of Switzerland."

So I have written for you these adventures of Anton and Trini, who live in the Alpland, where snow-capped mountains touch the clouds, where rushing waterfalls, tinkling cowbells, and sunny valleys make industrious Switzerland a place of beauty and song and summer flowers.

Virginia Olcott

STORIES ABOUT ANTON AND TRINI

"Anton carried the napkin tied to the alpenstock."

THAT SURPRISING LETTER FROM BERN

MOTHER RÄMI leaned over the balcony railing of the Swiss chalet on the mountain side. Little sister Dete was tugging at her apron. With one hand Mother Rämi held fast to Dete, while she waved the other toward the cheesery.

"Antonli! Antonli! Come here at once!" she called. The cheesery, where Father Rämi made such good cheese, was perched on the mountain slope below the chalet in which all the Rämis lived. It looked like a small log cabin, that cheesery. The walls of red pine-tree wood were built upon great, rough stones. One log was placed on another and others on that, and on the very top of all was a shingle roof. On the roof were laid black and white stones to keep it from blowing away.

1

The cattle shed stood close to the cheesery. It was a little, low hut of wood, its roof heaped with heavy stones covered with yellow and green moss. In this shed the two cows and three goats slept at night.

In the cheesery Father Rämi was making cheeses, and Anton, his son, ten years old, knelt on the cobble-stone floor scouring out a round wooden cheese vat.

2

As he scrubbed, Anton looked up at Father Rämi, who stood by a great copper kettle, pouring in the white, foaming milk from wooden milk pails. The kettle was almost as high as Anton. It hung from an iron hook on a tall wooden crane, over a fire burning on the stone floor. As each pail was emptied, Father Rämi stooped and stirred the kettle with a long ladle. Then the milk swished round the sides, and drops of foaming liquid flew up in the air like white rain.

"It is like the snowflakes when they blow down from our mountains," said Anton to himself. And then he heard his mother's voice calling:

"Antonli! Antonli! Come here at once!"

The father heard it too. He stopped stirring the kettle and said, "Hurry! The mother is calling."

Anton jumped up, still holding the scrubbing brush, and rushed out of the open door like the wind.

"What is the trouble, Mutterli?" he shouted. "Has Dete tumbled down again?"

He ran, out of breath, up the steep hillside toward the chalet. The straw brush still dripped white soapy water, as he climbed the outside stairs that led to the balcony.

Mother Rämi, smiling happily, took an envelope from her apron pocket, as she said, "Dete is quite well. But — here, read this!" Her eyes shone with delight as she added, "It's from Bern."

Bern was the fine city, the capital of Switzerland, that Mother Rämi was always talking about.

Anton sat cross-legged on the floor with his bare feet

3

tucked under him, while little sister Dete curled up in his lap. He opened the envelope with careful hands. Drawing out the letter, he unfolded it and read in clear, loud tones:

DEAR KLARA:

At last Trini and I can make you the promised visit. My husband has been ordered by the government to examine the roads in the cantons of Bern and Fribourg. While he is away, my little daughter and I will stay with you in your chalet. I shall see your fine boy, Anton, and wee Dete. And you will love my little Trini, I know. She is just nine years old and looks as I did when I lived with you and your dear father. How many years have passed since we last saw each other! Now we shall be together again, although your dear father is gone. On Saturday my Hans will bring us. Till then, dear Klara, I am

Your loving foster sister,
MATHILDE FASEL

Anton dropped the letter and looked up. Dete clapped her fat little hands; she knew that something nice had happened because Anton looked so pleased. And Mother Rämi kept whispering, "She is coming! Mathilde is truly coming!"

"Oh-ee!" Anton could not keep quiet a minute longer. He jumped to his feet and tossed Dete high in the air.

4

"Hear this, little Good-and-Sweet, you are going to have a big sister!"

Dete looked at him with round eyes. "Will she sing me a new song?" she asked.

"She will do all kinds of fine things. She lives in Bern," Anton cried. He set his little sister on the floor and hugged the precious letter. All the time he was thinking, "This is Thursday — Friday follows — and then Saturday comes!"

"Mutterli," said Anton at last, "they will be here in two days!"

Mother Rämi did not hear him. She stood leaning against the railing of the balcony, her eyes on the village lying in the green, sunny valley below. She thought of the days of her childhood. At that time Mathilde was an orphan, who lived in the house of Mother Rämi's father, and the two girls had grown up together like sisters. Then Mathilde had married the young engineer, Hans Fasel, and had moved to the old city of Bern. She, Mother Rämi, had married a young farmer in the village. Since then the foster sisters had not seen one another. But they had never forgotten the happy years spent in the village home in the valley.

Suddenly Mother Rämi remembered that she had many things to do before her guests arrived. The chalet, which Mathilde had never seen, must be put in spick-and-span order; fresh bread must be baked; and a new dress woven and stitched for Dete.

"Antonli," exclaimed Mother Rämi, "Saturday is almost here! There is work for each of us to do. Stack up the fallen logs under the eaves. But before you go, carry my loom out to the bench by the door, and when the church bell rings at sunset, come to supper."

With Dete hanging to her apron strings, the happy mother bustled out of the balcony into the house, and as she went she called out:

"Don't tell Father about the letter from Bern! We shall keep it as a surprise for supper time."

JOHANNLI'S AWFUL WORDS

ANTON still sat thinking on the floor of the balcony. Then he remembered his mother's orders and jumped to his feet. Off he bounded like a young goat. Soon the old wooden loom stood in the garden below, near the door of the chalet. Then he began to stack the pine logs to be used for fuel, under the eaves.

All the time Anton was thinking of Trini. He was glad school was over. In the mountain villages the schools closed at Easter, in order to let the boys and girls help in the fields and at home. Now he would have a playmate! That was a happy thought. He would be able to show Trini just how their tasty cheeses were made, and Anton smacked his lips. He would take her up into the hills and tell her the names of the flowers. So many things they would do together!

"She will be sure to like our house," he said to himself. "No other chalet on the mountains is so pretty as ours." Then he stood and looked with pride at their home.

Indeed, it was a lovely house, with its gay balcony and overhanging eaves of carved wood. It was built on the mountain slope, with meadows around it filled with yellow primroses and red anemones in summer time and heaped with glistening snow in winter. Back of the chalet loomed the high green mountains. They seemed to be touching the sky. Their tops glistened with snow that never melted and that grew fiery red at sunset time.

Today the chalet, in the clear May sunlight, with the birds singing in the pine trees that shaded its tall chimney, looked more beautiful than ever, Anton thought.

Father Rämi had often described to Anton the way in which many of the new chalets were built.

"In the old days," Father Rämi had told him, "we cut the wood in the forests ourselves, each neighbor helping the other to build the house. But now things are better. We Swiss are richer. Today, Antonli, if a man has the money, he can buy a beautiful wooden chalet made complete in the mills. Ours I bought from a famous mill in Geneva. In the mill yards our lovely chalet was planned, made, and put together. When it was finished the workmen took it down, piece by piece, and piled the parts upon a wagon drawn by oxen. Then they were carried up to this mountain slope, where they were put together again, beautiful and strong. The walls were set firmly on this cement foundation which you see here."

Yes, Anton knew that their house was strong. He remembered the terrible winter winds that swept down from the Alps. How hard they tried to shake and tear the chalet down! But they could not harm it. And the snow! How fast it piled up and froze into a heavy, crystal-blue coat all about the chalet's sides and on its shingled roof. Yet no drop of water or melted snow had ever leaked into their snug home.

Father Rämi was right in saying that the new chalets
were finer than the old ones. This one was so pretty!
Its walls were of unpainted wood, burned red and brown
by the hot sun. On the top of its roof, like a crown,

9

were more of the great black and white granite stones, which his father had brought from the mountain fields and placed on the chalet's roof to keep the shingles from blowing away.

The shingled roof slanted down toward the balcony, and its deep, golden-brown eaves reached out six feet into the air. And the balcony — what a happy place it was! It ran all around the house, with the eaves in summer making a cool, shady roof above it. There were flower boxes tucked in every corner, filled with mountain flowers in season: the wee rock-pansy, narcissus, wild violet, and slender nodding bluebell. In the early spring, when the snows first melted, the boxes were filled with white and yellow crocuses.

The railing of the balcony was covered with blossoms too — wooden ones! Father Rämi had carved in the wood trailing leaves and gentian flowers. And on the rail posts he had cut the heads of bears and wild turkeys. There was a door leading from the balcony into the bedrooms, and over it the father had carved in clear letters these words:

> May the good God watch
> over this house

It was two stories high, this chalet, and its many little windows were gay with flower boxes full of roses. And on both windows and boxes were carved rock-roses and

star-like edelweiss.   The edelweiss, you know, is the woolly little white flower with sage-green leaves that grows in the high Alps.

"Trini has never seen anything so fine as this house," Anton thought.   "No house in Bern can be quite so splendid."   And he began to work again, piling up the logs in neat rows beneath the eaves.

Anton had almost finished his task, when he heard a faint jingling of bells coming down the road that led to the pastures on the higher hills.   His eyes looked frightened.   He raised his head to listen.   A boy's voice was yodeling far up the road.   The yodeling came nearer, the bells jingled louder.

"It's almost sunset time," Anton said to himself, as he saw in the distance the long line of village cows coming home for the milking.

The cows had cream-white bodies with black spots. From each neck hung a brass or copper bell that jingled merrily.   At the cows' heels walked Johannli, the herd-boy.   He was waving a long ash stick and was poking the last cow to make her hurry along.

Johannli was a tall, thin boy. His face was as brown as a chestnut where the hot sunshine had burned it. His small eyes looked like bits of black coal. The sunshine falling on his head had bleached the ends of his long, straight hair till they were almost white.

He wore a white shirt and a gay red vest with gilt buttons. Nodding from his round black cap was a spray of sky-blue gentian buds that he had gathered on the mountain side. Those sweet flowers were the only attractive things that Johannli had about him, for his face was always scowling and his mouth hateful.

Anton was a little afraid of the herdboy. Often, when Johannli passed the Rämi's house with the cows, he threw stones at Anton or whisked his bare feet with the ash stick.

Johannli now stopped before the chalet to let the two great black and white spotted cows that belonged to Father Rämi leave the herd and go to their shed. He blew his short alphorn, and all the animals stood still at once. Father Rämi's cows knew that this was their home. They separated themselves from the other cows and, swishing their tails, went slowly toward the cheesery and the cattle hut, where Father Rämi was waiting to milk them.

Anton worked harder than ever piling up the logs, thinking all the time of the ash stick. Johannli came close to him and asked rudely, "What are you doing?"

"Stacking wood. Can't you see?" answered Anton.

"Why?" and the herdboy poked him with his stick.

"Trini is coming." Anton did not move. He would not let Johannli know that he was afraid.

"Who is Trini?" The stick pricked Anton's bare feet.

"She is a girl!" Anton wanted to finish his task before the church bell rang, and wished that Johannli would not ask so many questions. But Johannli spoke again:

"A girl! I shall not like her."

It was Anton's turn to ask a question. He dropped the wood and bravely faced the scowling herdboy. "Why?" he demanded.

"Girls are silly, proud things—they can't climb the rocks, they can't jump a crack in a glacier, they can't yodel—they're idiots!" and Johannli squinted his small eyes.

"Trini's not proud! She's not silly! She comes from Bern," cried Anton, and turned his back on Johannli.

The village cows were tired of waiting; they wanted to go to their sheds. They began to shake their heads restlessly and to moo; the bells jingled and the herdboy went at once to his charges. But as he led them off, he shouted:

"I shall see your Trini from Bern. She will hold her silly head high and strut like a pigeon."

Then the cows went jingling down the slope to the town, with Johannli following after, yodeling as he went.

TRINI IS COMING!

As Johannli went down the hill, Anton sat on the grass and hugged his bare knees.   He wanted to cry with disappointment.   He never had seen Trini — it was true! Perhaps Johannli was right after all.   Perhaps she was proud and would not like his chalet.   The fine plans that he had been making vanished.   He did not want to play all summer with a girl who strutted like a pigeon.

Then from the church in the village sounded the chiming bells, telling the herdsmen and workers in the fields that it was the sunset hour and time to go to their homes and rest.   Anton placed the last log on the high pile and went slowly into the house.

15

"It is all finished, Mutterli, that woodpile," he said soberly.

Mother Rämi was standing by the table pouring sweet fresh milk into four blue bowls. The bowls were the delight of her heart. They were decorated with a pattern of lovely edelweiss like rows of velvety white flowers. She had bought those bowls when she first moved into this new chalet.

At the sound of Anton's unhappy voice, she turned so quickly that one of the bowls upset. The milk went trickling down the red tablecloth and fell in a puddle on the clean floor.

"What is this?" Mother Rämi cried. "You come in with a voice like a lost goat! The milk spills everywhere, and my lovely bowl is almost broken to bits! There has been enough excitement today without this trouble."

She began to mop up the milk, but when she saw the boy's miserable face, she spoke kindly. "What is the matter, Antonli?"

"Mutterli, is Trini a silly, proud girl?"

Mother Rämi began to laugh.

"Is that what is troubling you? No, no! If Trini is at all like her mother, she'll be a fine playmate and a sweet little friend."

This gave Anton cheer. Surely his mother was wiser than Johannli. She knew everything, and Johannli had not even been to school for the last three years. He was always up in the hills with the cows.

Anton went and stood by the table and touched a

bowl. Trini could borrow his, he thought. She would like the pretty clay edelweiss that circled round its edge, he felt sure.

"Now," said the mother as she filled the empty bowl, "it is time for your father. Then we shall tell him about the surprise."

She went to the stove and took out a platter of whole-wheat bread spread with toasted cheese and put it on the table. How good it smelled! Anton stood and looked at it and sniffed. He forgot his miserable thoughts about Trini and sat beside Dete on the bench before the table.

The door opened. Father Rämi came into the room.

"Vaterli! A surprise! There is a surprise coming!" Anton darted to him and took the wooden milk pail he carried.

"Ho, there, little Sparrow!" Father Rämi ruffled up the boy's yellow curls as he spoke. "Have you eaten all my supper, to surprise my hungry stomach?"

Anton put the pail of fresh milk in one corner of the room, while his father sat down in the big chair near the table. Anton ran back to his place on the bench. Mother Rämi sat near him, with Dete on her knees, and served the family.

What a happy supper! They all had fine appetites. Soon bowls and platters were empty. Then Mother Rämi drew out the envelope from her apron pocket.

"What is this?" asked Father Rämi.

"Tell him, Mutterli! Tell the surprise!" Anton cried.

Dete clapped both hands on the mother's cheeks, as Mother Rämi told the wonderful news the letter had brought from Bern that afternoon.

"So Mathilde is coming after all," said Father Rämi.

"Yes, Mathilde is coming at last," said Mother Rämi.

"Trini is coming!" shouted Anton at the top of his voice. He had forgotten Johannli's awful words.

Dete tried to speak; instead she squeaked and dropped her sleepy little head on her mother's shoulder and went fast asleep. The mother rocked her softly and sang the lullaby that all Swiss children love:

"Sleep, baby, sleep!
Thy father tends the sheep!
Thy mother shakes the little tree;
A tiny dream falls down on thee.
Sleep, baby, sleep!"

Evening came on. The little chalet was filled with shadows. Suddenly a great wind swept down from the mountains. The old pine tree outside the house swayed, shook, and sighed, as though it would break in two. The quiet room was filled with the rushing noise of its bending branches.

"Time to sleep, Antonli," Father Rämi yawned.

Anton looked up at the carved wooden clock that hung on the wall. Just then its wooden cuckoo-bird put out a gilt head from the wee door of the clock and called *cuckoo! cuckoo!* seven times, while little bells inside tinkled seven merry notes.

Anton climbed the narrow stairway to the rooms above. In a few minutes he was curled up in his hard bed beneath the window. Again he thought of Johannli's words, and as he watched the shining moon above the distant mountain tops, he was sure he saw a little girl walk over the moon-hills, holding her head high and strutting like a pigeon—then he was asleep.

19

WAS JOHANNLI RIGHT?

"THEY are coming, Mutterli!" It was Saturday noon, and Anton stood at the door waiting eagerly. A big automobile filled with boxes and suitcases and a bird cage, with Father and Mother Fasel and Trini, was driving up to the Rämi's chalet.

How golden bright was the sun! How blue was the May sky! The birds and the trees seemed to know that something specially nice had come to their home; the birds sang, and the fir trees swayed and murmured fragrant greetings to Trini.

Mother Rämi, with her arms about Mother Fasel, hurried into the house. Father Rämi and Father Fasel stood together admiring the new automobile.

And Trini? She jumped out of the machine with one hand holding a gilt bird cage, while the other clasped tight to her breast a handkerchief which wriggled and squirmed.

Anton knew at once that she was not proud, but— she might be silly! Her little head was tied in a pink hood, with yellow curls peeping from beneath its ruffles. Her cheeks were pink, with dimples twinkling in and out. She looked like a happy, sweet-tempered girl.

"Here!" she called to Anton, as she danced over to him on the tips of her quick feet. "Here is my family for us to play with!"

She sat on the grass and put down the bird cage, carefully unwinding the dark cloth tied round its side. In
the cage was a swallow.

Then Trini opened the wriggling handkerchief, and
out came a gray kitten.

"*Her* name is Sausage," Trini said, stroking the kitten, "because she is so fat. And *her* name is the Traveler"— Trini pointed to the bird cage. "Last year she went to Greece."

"How do you know that?" asked Anton. He sat down near her and poked a bit of grass through the wires at the swallow.

"Last summer," said Trini, "she made her nest in the eaves of our house, just over the door. We caught her and tied a note to her leg. On the note we wrote, WHERE ARE YOU GOING THIS WINTER? Then we let her fly away."

"Where did she go?" Anton was anxious to hear everything.

"She went to Greece," said Trini. "She flew back to her nest over our door in the spring, and there was another note tied to her leg. Someone had written, I HAVE BEEN IN ATHENS ALL WINTER. And so she is called the Traveler."

"She must be a wise old bird," Anton said. "She is like our storks. They come to Fribourg in the spring and go to Greece and Egypt in the winter. They are travelers too."

Trini hopped from the ground. She picked up the cage and caught the kitten by the nape of her neck, crying, "Let us both be travelers! Now! Where shall we go?"

That idea pleased Anton. "Let us go to the pastures," he cried.

"Come, let us go quickly," exclaimed happy little Trini. And together they ran into the chalet, calling out to their mothers, "We are travelers! We shall leave our family here and go into the hills."

Mother Fasel set the cage on the table. Little Dete and the kitten crept into a corner to play. Mother Rämi wrapped big pieces of bread and cheese and some ginger cake in a large napkin.

"Here," said she to Anton, "eat your dinner when you are hungry, and bring Trini safely home at sunset."

Anton took his alpenstock from behind the stove and looked for Trini. He tapped the long stick on the floor impatiently. Trini was too busy to hear. That morning, as she came from Bern, she had seen country children on the roads, barefooted. In the city Trini always wore high boots, but now that she was a country girl, off must go her shoes! In a moment she stood barefooted in front of her mother, shouting, "All summer, Mutterli, I shall not wear my boots! I want to be just like Antonli."

Then the two children ran out of the house.

Anton was saying to himself, "Trini is not proud! She is a girl, and she walks like a strong boy — she doesn't strut like a pigeon. Johannli was wrong!"

THE BEARS OF BERN

THE two children climbed nimble-footed up the mountain pass. Anton carried the napkin carefully knotted and tied to the alpenstock, which he held over his shoulder. Trini, like a graceful little wild kid, skipped along on her bare feet in the soft grass. She was bold and daring. She darted here and there, gathering clusters of gay flowers. She stepped more carefully

24

among the stones and rocks, for she was not used to going without shoes.

The great cliffs and lonely mountains delighted her. She stood still suddenly on a giant stone that lay in their path and stretched out both her arms.

"Watch the clouds," she cried. "They float in the sky just as the little boats float on the river Aare in Bern!"

Anton wanted to hear all about Bern. So, as they climbed farther up the hill to reach the pasture land where Johannli watched the village herd, Trini told him stories that her father had told her about the city of Bern.

"Bern is the capital of our country," said Trini proudly, "and in Bern we have bears everywhere."

"Bears!" cried Anton.

"Not live ones. But the figures of bears are on our flags, on our door knockers, and carved on the eaves and trimmings of our houses. And on the old Clock Tower there is a troop of little bears that run in a circle whenever the clock strikes the hour. And we have gingerbread bears at the bakers."

"Why do you have bears?" asked Anton. "Why don't you have the figure of our mountain eagle or one of our lovely cows?"

Trini nodded. "Yes," she said, "our cows are beautiful. But the emblem of Bern is the bear. *Bern* means "bear"! And on the banks of the Aare, there is a bear's den with real live bears in it — brown, fluffy ones."

Trini sat down to rest as she said that, and Anton listened with round eyes.

"Father takes me every holiday to see them. Last week we leaned over the rail to watch them, and I saw the mother bear spank the baby bear."

"Oh, what a lie!" exclaimed Anton. Yet he wanted to go to Bern, to see if it were true. He wanted to see for himself the city which held so many wonderful things.

"It is true!" Trini cried. She sat up straight and glared at him.

"Never mind what I said," said Anton humbly. "Tell me more."

Trini laughed and soon was telling him all about the river Aare winding through the city — of the old bridges, and towers, and gates, and the many shining mountains.

"The fountain that I like best," said Trini, "is the one which was built by the old musicians of Bern. We call it the Bagpipe Fountain, for it is the figure of a man playing a bagpipe. He has a monkey by him, and a goose, and his toes are out of his shoes; but he does not care, for his pipes seem to be making such a glad noise."

Anton sighed. He had never been to a large city. He wished he could see some of the grand sights that Trini saw every day when she was at home. For the first time he did not love to look at the beautiful mountains around his chalet.

But Trini did. For a while she sat perfectly still, gazing up at the mountains that loomed far above, the sun's golden light tingeing their snow-tops with rosy colors.

27

"Oh!" cried the little girl, "Bern is beautiful, but I would rather live here among the hills. We can see the Alps from our city, but they are far off. Up here we are a part of the mountains." And she jumped up and began to dance on.

Suddenly she darted forward. They had reached a stretch of lovely grass, pink with primroses and set with swaying fir trees. Nestled among the trees was a little wooden hut, dark brown like burnt bread crust, with deep, fringed eaves and a tall chimney on one side. Over the door was carved in the brown wood:

> Joyous be the outlook of this little
> Swiss house on the alp=world

"Oh!" cried Trini, pointing to the wee hut. "Who lives in that dolly's house?"

"A doll's house!" exclaimed Anton in scorn. "Why, old Father Fly Eyes lives there. We call him that, for his eyes are so sharp and bright they see everything. He sees as much with his two eyes as a fly does with its dozens. And—there he is now!"

As he spoke, a tall old man came to the door of the house. He stepped outside and sat down on a low bench by the open door, and began to work on something which he held in his hands.

"What is he doing?" Trini asked. She caught Anton's hand and started to run toward the hut.

As she ran with twinkling feet and curls bobbing, Anton sprang along by her side. He held tight to her hand and said to himself, "How surprised Johannli would be to see a girl climbing the rocks as fast as a boy."

Trini stopped a few paces from the hut and stood looking at the old man. He nodded when he saw the children, and called out pleasantly, "Good day, Antonli! Have you come to pay me a visit?"

Father Fly Eyes was as tall and straight as a fir tree. His hair was very long and very white. On the top of his head was a leather hat with little metal figures of flowers and animals round its crown. He wore an old dark coat and short leather trousers and red woolen stockings.

Trini looked carefully at his eyes. She had never seen anything like those eyes. They were blue, as deep blue and clear as icicles on a blue-sky day. His face was lined with hundreds of tiny wrinkles, while his chin was long and pointed like the chin of a good fairy.

"Have you come to pay me a visit?" he said again; and holding out a piece of wood carved into the shape of a little animal like a small mountain deer, he asked, "How do you like this?"

The two children drew close to the bench to examine the piece of carved work. It was a figure of a goat-antelope, the little Alpine mountain chamois, slender and bounding on its long, straight legs. Its two horns were curved gracefully backward. Its two ears were pointed as though it were listening. About its neck was hanging

29

a wreath of edelweiss. The eyes, the hair, the delicate nostrils of the tiny animal were so finely cut in the wood that the figure seemed alive.

"Oh, see the chamois!" cried Anton.

Trini's eyes shone, and she stroked the little wooden animal with happy hands. That pleased the old wood-carver.

"Come," he said, and getting up stiffly from the bench, led the two children into the hut.

THE WONDERS OF WOOD

THE little hut was dark. It was just one small, dusty room. It had only a low bed, a square table, a chair, and a stove for furniture. There were shelves all along its walls of unpainted boards. Long shelves and little deep shelves were cut into the walls like steps. And on the shelves were piled all kinds of carved wooden wonders.

The children could not take their eyes away from those shelves. One was filled with wooden toys, stiff little wooden dolls, dainty chalets with low carved eaves and tiny shingled roofs, and long, fine whips, their handles decorated with the heads of eagles. The other shelves held wooden book-ends, wooden ink bottles, wooden mugs with handles entwined with leaves, and many beautiful boxes — little boxes and big boxes, and each with a different design cut into the wood. And on the walls of the hut hung eight cuckoo clocks.

"Now," said Father Fly Eyes, "what do you think of these?" and he waved his long hand toward the shelves.

"Oh!" Trini cried. "This is the most wonderful house in Switzerland! Antonli, look! Look at those wooden shoes!" She pointed to a pair of real wooden shoes that stood on a low shelf.

Father Fly Eyes nodded happily.

31

"Yes, yes," he said and patted Trini's curls. "This child is wise. She knows the worth of wood." He took down the shoes and held them out to her. "Put them on," he said.

Trini sat on the hard stone floor and slipped her bare feet into the shoes. Then she stood up and began to walk. *Clip-clap, clip-clap* they went against the stones.

32

"What beautiful music they make!" she said. "Do you keep all these lovely things to play with?"

At this the old man laughed.

"No," answered he, "I carry them twice a year to the nearest towns. The many foreigners who come there buy my wooden things to take back to their own lands. So I sell them in the towns to shopkeepers, who pay me money for them. With that money I buy my bread."

"How rich you must be!" Anton said. "You must get many francs for such lovely things." He held up a tall wooden figure of a milkmaid with her pail. She was a peasant woman from another part of Switzerland, dressed in the quaint clothes of her district. Her carved wooden skirt and apron seemed real. On her head a wooden cap stood out like butterfly wings. Her tiny milk pail was exactly like the big pails that hung in Father Rämi's cheesery.

The old wood-carver took the figure and looked at it lovingly.

"No, no, Antonli!" he said sadly. "In past years I made money with my dear wooden pieces. But today it is different. There are too many factories and big shops where they make wooden things by machinery. My beautiful hand-carved pieces are not bought as they used to be."

"Father Fly Eyes! Father Fly Eyes!" Trini called. She clattered over in the wooden shoes and pointed to where a wooden bear sat on a shelf above the stove. "Father Fly Eyes, there is our bear from Bern!"

"Yes, little Wise One, that is the bear of your city," the old man answered. "And there is the Lion of Lucerne." He held up, as he spoke, a wooden figure of a lion pierced with a lance, lying with his great paw on a shield.

"What do you know about Lucerne and this old lion?" he asked them suddenly, looking sharply at Anton, his blue eyes glinting.

"Tell us!" said Anton.

"Tell us!" begged Trini. She caught the old man's hand and pulled him toward the chair. "Tell us a story of Lucerne. Please tell us about Switzerland."

"No, no! It is long past midday," Father Fly Eyes answered. "I must get my dinner."

"No, no! You must tell us a story," pleaded both the children together, "and we have the dinner — here — in our napkin."

Anton quickly took the napkin from the end of his stick and unwrapped it.

There were great pieces of mellow, rich cheese and soft, crusty bread, and big hunks of golden-yellow ginger cake which Mother Rämi had baked that morning. There was enough for *five* hungry people!

And what a happy feast they had in the little brown hut! Anton thought that whole-wheat bread the finest in the world. Trini knew she had never tasted better cheese. Father Rämi's cows, living on juicy grasses, sweet-scented herbs, and glacier-pure water, had given the delicious milk from which that cheese was made.

But the old wood-carver could not say enough in praise of the ginger cake. Father Fly Eyes, living alone among the hills, had no money to buy sweets; and Mother Rämi's ginger cake was the richest cake in the world to him.

And when they had finished every crumb of the dinner, Father Fly Eyes said, "Come, we will sit outside, and I will tell you about our country."

With the warm May sun shining above them and the fir trees casting shade on the little hut, all three sat on the bench by the door while the old wood-carver told them of Switzerland, of its snows, glaciers, and avalanches, of its turquoise lakes and quaint old cities.

STORIES FATHER FLY EYES TELLS

"ONCE upon a time, long, long ago, in our mountains, foothills, lakelands, and valleys lived the Helvetian people.

"The Helvetians liked the lakelands and valleys better than the wild mountains, and they built villages and towns in the plains and round the shores of our lakes. Some of our big cities today are on the sites of those Helvetian towns. Geneva, by the rushing Rhone; Lausanne, on the slopes of Mount Jorat; and Zurich-on-the-Lake, guarded by the towering snow-covered Alps, were all once Helvetian towns.

"In time the Helvetians were conquered by the powerful Romans, the people living in the land we call Italy. Then other peoples came, from the land now called Germany, and from the land now called France. These peoples brought into Switzerland their own languages.

"So today in Switzerland we speak four languages: French in some of our cantons — cantons are Swiss states, you know — German in others, and Italian in others; while Romansch — a language much like Latin — is spoken in some of our valleys. But although we folk in Switzerland speak several languages, our hearts are Swiss. We all love our country and our crimson flag with the pure white cross."

When Trini heard this, she jumped up and clapped her hands, shouting, "Now I know! Now I know!"

"What do you know, little Wise One?" asked Father Fly Eyes, smiling at the excited child.

"Why, that's the reason, when Mutterli sends me to Mother Gutknechts's bakeshop, she tells me to speak German," said Trini thoughtfully; "and when she sends me to Mother Chaillet's shop for cheese and butter, she tells me to speak French. Though their stores are on the same street, they each speak a different language; yet they are both Swiss."

"Yes, yes, there are many French-speaking Swiss and German-speaking Swiss in old Bern," replied the wood-carver. Then he turned to Anton, who sat wide-eyed, listening, and asked, "Tell me, Antonli, what languages do we speak in our canton of Fribourg?"

Anton knew. "Most of the people speak French," he answered at once and pointed to the distant Jura mountain range. "France lies very near us over there, but some speak German — my father does."

"And the Lion, tell us about the Lion of Lucerne!" Trini tugged at the old man's sleeve.

"That old Lion honors our Swiss Guards, the loyal soldiers who died trying to save the life of the French King over a hundred years ago," said Father Fly Eyes. "And when you go to Lucerne, you will find that Lion of Lucerne carved on the face of a great rock. You will see a silvery, singing brook at the foot of the cliff, and beautiful trees shading it. And in the center of the

37

cliff you will see the dying Lion reaching out his great
paw to guard the shield of France."

"We have bears in Bern," said Trini proudly, "but no
lions."

"And we have chamois bounding up and down our
hills here, and heath cocks," said Anton, "but no lions."

"There are some other wonderful things guarding Lucerne," said the wood-carver, smiling down at them both.

"What? What?" cried the children.

"Royal mountains," answered the wood-carver. "Some
are snow-clad and rugged and fearful; others, covered

with flowers in summer, and with greenest trees almost to their summits. These are the guardian mountains of Lucerne."

"What are the guardian mountains of Bern?" Trini asked. She loved her home city and wanted to know everything that helped to make it beautiful and famous.

"The tallest Swiss mountains are far from Bern," replied Father Fly Eyes. Then, as he saw her disappointed face, he added, "but our Swiss railways go up near the crests and peaks of the Bernese Alps. Our steam and electric engines rush bravely through long tunnels. They cross terrible passes and valley crags on strongly built bridges. And our railways climb up the steepest mountain side, thousands of feet into the air. So visitors from all over the world come to Bern, and from there they go up into the mountains."

That pleased Trini. She sat still a moment, thinking of her home. But Anton wanted to know more.

"Vaterli goes to Geneva every spring to sell the cowharnesses which he has made during the winter. When he comes home, he tells me about a wonderful mountain that he has seen when the skies are clear."

"Yes, yes, that is Mont Blanc, the White Mountain!" exclaimed Father Fly Eyes. "Antonli, everywhere you look in Switzerland there are mountains. High mountains, standing alone, seeming to touch the sky — long mountain ranges with snow-capped peaks — low sweeping mountains stretching down into the valleys, but Mont Blanc is the highest of them all."

39

Then he pointed to the meadow before him, carpeted with yellow violets, pink primroses, and clusters of white narcissus, and said:

"Although we have mountains everywhere in our country, look at these flowers, see those forest trees higher up on the mountain. Our little country is very rich and blessed in growing things. Our summer pasture lands feed our cows and herds. Our forest lands drain and clean our soil and give us wood and timber for our houses; they protect us, too, from the fierce snow avalanches which might rush down the mountain sides and destroy our homes. And our meadow lands grow splendid crops of potatoes and beets and all the grains."

The cowbells tinkled on the hills above, and the merry sound came nearer. The afternoon hours had slipped away while the children were listening to the stories.

"What is this?" exclaimed Father Fly Eyes. "The sun is setting! Here I am wasting the hours, when I should be using my tools. Go home, children, go home at once!" and he clapped his hands together as if shooing chickens.

Trini and Anton looked up at the mountain tops where the sun was sinking. The green of the slopes had changed to rosy gold, and the tops of the mountains where the snow lay were tinted cherry color.

"Oh!" cried Anton. "It is almost time for supper!" He caught Trini by the hand, and they both started to run down the mountain side.

Trini had forgotten that she was still wearing the

40

wooden shoes.　In a moment her foot hit a rock.　With a crash she stumbled and fell to the ground.　Both the shoes jumped from her feet.　Rubbing her bare knees and puckering her face into a knot, she picked up the shoes and started to carry them back to the hut.

But old Father Fly Eyes, watching from the doorway, called to her:

"Take them home, little Wise One.　I ate your fine dinner, and you may wear my wooden shoes back to Bern."

TRINI–NEVER–AFRAID

DOWN the mountain side the children ran fast. Trini hugged the wooden shoes close to her breast. She was thinking how pleased her mother would be to see them, with the wreath of wee gentian buds carved on the top of each shoe. And Anton was thinking that his blue bowl of fresh milk would seem the nicest thing in the world.

The church bell was ringing in the village, from the higher hills the alphorns were echoing, and the high, changing voices of the herdsmen's yodel sounded clearly above all the chiming music. The light began to fade and twilight fell.

Then the jingling bells sounded close by, and behind the children trooped the village cows with Johannli following and swinging his ash stick.

"Here come the cows—and Johannli," Anton said anxiously. He stepped to one side of the path to let the herd pass.

But Trini was pleased with the sight of the cattle and their tinkling bells. She stood in the middle of the road and called, "Come to me, you pretty, dear things! Come to me!"

The big cow that led the herd was startled to see Trini standing in her pathway. She wanted to get to her shed to be milked. With an angry "Moo-oo-oo," she put down her big horned head and went crossly toward the child, while the other cows pushed forward with clattering hoofs and jingling bells.

"Run, Trini, run!" shouted Anton, wildly trying to reach her, but he could not push past the crowding cows.

Trini, who had never been afraid in her life, stood still and waited as the black and white cow came toward her. She did not know the cow was angry. The animal was startled at the little figure that did not move. Suddenly the cow stopped, then quietly walked to one side of the path and passed her. The other cows followed.

43

And Johannli? He was so surprised at Trini's daring
that he could not move. When his cows had gone down
the road, he rubbed his eyes and stared at the little girl.

"Are you Trini from Bern?" he snapped.

Trini nodded cheerfully. She was interested in
Johannli's queer, gnarled face. His cap had fallen off,
and his long, yellow hair with white ends hanging close
to his cheeks made his tanned face seem almost black.
His small eyes shone like black coals. She had never seen
such a strange-looking boy.

Anton remembered what Johannli had said to him the night before. He ran up to the herdboy and shouted, "Does she strut like a pigeon? Is she proud? Do you like her?"

Johannli picked up his cap. Waving his ash stick and shaking his head, he moved away sullenly, calling to Anton as he went, "Silly! Silly! Silly!"

Then he ran after his cows.

In the chalet Mother Rämi and Mother Fasel were waiting for the children. Supper was waiting too. It stood on the table, steaming hot — potatoes, boiled white as down; hunks of toasted cheese; and, in honor of the visitors, a fine leg of roasted mutton.

Trini rushed into the room, holding out the wooden shoes and calling, "Look! Look at what Father Fly Eyes gave me."

And Anton added, "The cows tried to scare Trini, and she wasn't afraid."

Then, while the family ate supper, Anton told their adventures in the hills, and Father Fasel said proudly, "Yes, our Trini is brave! But why not? Doesn't she see bears every day in Bern?"

OFF TO GENEVA

Fast the spring days flew! Each one was filled with exciting good times for Anton and Trini.

There was work for the children as well as play. Anton helped in the cheesery. Each morning he scrubbed out the round cheese vats and the wooden milk pails. He helped to plant the potatoes and other vegetables in the garden patch, which lay at one side of the cattle shed. He fed the chickens. He brought in the wood, stacked beneath the eaves, for the kitchen fire. And he tended the three goats, which were not sent to the pastures with the cows.

Trini worked too. She dressed little Dete and sang

her to sleep after the daily bath in the big iron tub. She gathered the eggs from the hens' nests in the shed. And Mother Rämi taught her to iron the stiff, starched window curtains, their edges fringed with homemade lace. Then there was the Traveler to be fed a daily feast of bread crumbs, and Sausage to wash and comb. All this was work that Trini loved to do.

One sunny morning Anton and Trini sat on the bench outside the chalet door, eating a breakfast of bread and wild-strawberry jam. Dete was there too, drinking fresh milk from one of the blue bowls, while Sausage lapped up cream from a plate on the ground.

Toot! toot! toot! They suddenly heard the sound of Father Fasel's automobile coming up the slope. He had been away for three days, examining the roads on the hills and in the valleys of the canton of Fribourg.

"Vaterli is here!" and Trini darted toward the car, which had driven up to the house.

"Ho, there, pretty Alpine Röschen!" Father Fasel said, as the little girl scrambled into the car and perched on his lap. Then he called out, "Antonli, would you like to go to Geneva?"

Like to go to Geneva! Anton jumped up from the bench. Would he like to go to Geneva! There was no other city in the world that he wanted so much to see.

Father Fasel was busy with the engine of his car, and, without waiting for an answer, he spoke again. "Be off, both of you, and tell the mothers that I am going to take you away for the day."

The children rushed into the house and in a few minutes returned. Trini wore the pink hood and coat and the stiff boots that she had on when she came from Bern. Anton followed her. He was dressed in his Easter clothes. He wore a white shirt and a pair of long brown trousers. On his head was a white straw hat. He walked stiffly; his feet hurt, squeezed into shoes which he wore only on Sundays and holidays.

"We are ready to go!" they cried and climbed into the car. The mothers came to the door and waved goodbye as the automobile sped down the mountain slope toward Geneva, the famous city on the shores of the Lake of Geneva, seventy miles away.

Anton was too excited to speak. He sat in the back seat of the car next to Trini. His eyes were fixed on his boots, and he was thinking. He was going to Geneva at last. He was going to see the famous city which had seven bridges. He was going to see the White Mountain.

But Trini could not keep still. She jumped down from the seat and pressed her face to the window as the car wound its way among the hills and down into the valleys. Every minute she called to her father, "Vaterli, what is that we are passing?"

"That's a vineyard where grapes grow," answered Father Fasel.

Then the car whizzed past and left the lovely green slope covered with grapevines far away.

"Vaterli, what is that we are passing?"

"That's the ruins of an old castle where barons lived
long ago," Father Fasel replied, and drove the car slowly
so that the children might look at the old gray castle on
the hill, with its towers clothed in ivy, gazing proudly
down on the valleys below it.

How beautiful was that ride through the Gruyère
valleys! They crossed rich, delicious pastures, where
cows browsed among juicy herbs and tender grasses, feast-
ing to make the perfumed milk from which the Gruyère
cheese is made.   What splendid cows they were — heavy
black and white beasts with delicate pink nostrils and
deep, soft eyes!

Now and then a little squirrel perched on a chestnut
bough, its tail raised like a waving plume, and chattered
as the car went by.   Mountain butterflies with rose-
petal wings fluttered in the sunny roadway.

Then they passed the walled town of Gruyères, planted on a high hill. Anton and Trini peered out of the window at the castle on the top of the hill. They could see quite plainly its towers, its pointed roofs and old sentry gate, and the steep road paved with huge pebbles which led up to it.

As they rode on, Father Fasel told the children of the quaint old town of Gruyères.

"There is only one street in Gruyères," Father Fasel told them. "The castle is on that street, and so are all the little white-eaved homes with benches before their doors and geranium flowers on their window sills. It is called 'The Street,' for there is no other."

While Father Fasel was talking, the car sped away from Gruyères, and soon the round castle tower, looking like a gray bird on the hill, disappeared altogether.

How fast the car went! Suddenly the children saw a patch of blue in the distance. It grew larger and larger. It was the Lake of Geneva.

They rode through the small towns that lay along the borders of the lake. Whenever the car was close to the lake shore, Anton pressed his face to the window. He loved to watch the boats with flapping lateen sails float over the water like giant butterflies. Trini gave little purrs of joy at the sight of the old houses with gables and brown-green eaves, tall chimneys, outside stairs, and wooden balconies.

At midday they reached the beautiful City of Seven Bridges — Geneva.

THE GIANT OF MONT BLANC

"THIS is the Street of the White Mountain," Father Fasel said.

He steered his car carefully down one of the main streets of Geneva. The Street of the White Mountain was broad and sloped gradually down to the lake. It was alive with motor cars, carriages, and trolleys. People were walking to and fro.

There were beautiful, lofty buildings on both sides of the street. But the one that delighted the children most was the post office, standing near the English church. It was tall and glittering white in the sunlight. Statues stood on the high edge of its roof, perched like birds ready to fly away.

"There is Mont Blanc!" Father Fasel stopped the car and pointed to where the great mountain loomed in the distance.

"O-o-oh!" Anton's voice could scarcely be heard. But Trini cried out:

"It's a giant! It's a giant! His head is covered with snow."

Father Fasel laughed. "Yes," he replied, "it is a giant mountain. You are fortunate to see it at all. It usually hides away among the clouds. And now," said he, "let us eat our dinner"; and he drove the automobile down a side street to a restaurant.

The long ride in the hills and the bracing mountain air had given them a fine appetite. Anton ate everything in every dish set before him. Golden fried fish, chicken stew, omelette, crusty little rolls, fat chocolate puffs vanished into his mouth as fast as they were offered him.

Trini drank her hot chocolate and nibbled rolls quietly for a moment, then said coaxingly, "Vaterli, tell us a story of the White Mountain."

Father Fasel had finished his dinner. While Anton still ate, he leaned back in his chair and told the old folk story that Swiss children love to hear.

"Once upon a time," said Father Fasel, "in this land of lakes and Alps, giants dwelt in the mists that drift around the mountain tops.

"These huge creatures strode to and fro among the peaks, now shouting in voices like thunder, now rolling avalanches of rocks and snow down into the valleys beneath. Sometimes they threw rocks crashing down the sides of the mountains. But the giants were really good-tempered and did not wish to harm anyone.

"Where Mont Blanc rears its ice-clad head among the clouds, once lived a grand old giant. He was so tremendous that when he sat down upon the top of Mont Blanc, his feet hung over into the valleys. When he slept, his snores sounded like the roar of avalanches, and the folk in the valleys trembled for fear the fall of avalanches might bury them alive. When he pillowed his head on a peak, his white beard, thick and spreading, hung down the sides of the mountain, looking like new-fallen snow. As for his great sunken eyes, the folk below thought them caverns, and his mouth they took for a wide crevasse in a glacier.

"One day this good old giant lay down for a little nap. It happened that on the mountain side a herd of cows was feeding. As the cows wandered about, they came to what looked like a pleasant red cave. They sauntered in and began to walk down a red lane. Ha! ha! ha! The giant felt them tickling, for they were in his mouth, of course, and were walking down his throat. He woke.

"He gave one long cough, and *poof!* the cows went

sailing out of his mouth, through the air miles away, and *poof!* they landed gently in another country. Ha! ha! ha!

"That," said Father Fasel, "is the end of my story." And he added, laughing, "Antonli, if you eat another mouthful of food, you will grow as big as that giant."

Trini slipped from her chair with a roll in one hand. "I shall take this home to the Traveler," said she, "it's so good!" and she tucked it in the pocket of her coat.

"Come," said Father Fasel, and led them out to the automobile. "Now I shall show you a part of this beautiful city," said he as he drove along the streets.

They crossed one of the seven bridges over the "blue water of the arrowy Rhone," and drove to the Promenade of Bastions close by the great University. As they were driving down a street, Trini suddenly cried out, "What is that, Vaterli?" and tugged at Father Fasel's arm.

"Be careful, little daughter! Remember that I am driving!" exclaimed the father.

"Over there! That house! Those children!" cried Trini.

They were passing a large house, a dignified old house, and to it was fastened a brass plate, on which were the words:

ÉCOLE INTERNATIONALE

Groups of children were going in. They were not Swiss, those children. One little girl had long, flaxen braids and big, china-blue eyes, and she was chattering in a strange language. Another was olive-skinned, graceful, swaying, with large, sparkling black eyes. One boy was short, with slanting eyes like almonds, and a flat nose. Another was a young giant, broad-shouldered, and foreign in his talk. There were many boys and girls, a hundred or more, dark or light, and of all sizes. And they were talking and laughing in many languages.

"It is a school," said Anton.

"Yes," answered Father Fasel, "and the most wonderful school in the world, the International School. Those are 'Peace children.' They come from many countries, and their fathers are attending the Peace Conference of the League of Nations. Did you see that little Chinese girl? And the Czech boy? And the Lithuanian little one?"

"I think I saw an English girl and a French one," cried Trini.

"I am sure that big boy was a Norwegian," exclaimed Anton, "and the tall one with red hair was a Finn."

"Tell us about the League of Nations, Vaterli," begged Trini.

"Not today," said Father Fasel, "I have not even time to take you to the airdrome, from which the airplanes start for Zurich." Then he stopped the car near the quay, where the rushing River Rhone divided the city into two parts, and said, "I have business to do. I shall leave you two here. Play around till I return. Do not go into the city."

Then away he drove and left the children standing on the long quay — the broad walk that lined the shore.

THE ISLAND OF BIRDS

Anton and Trini stood on the long walk and looked across the water. It was three o'clock. The mid-afternoon sun shone brightly on the broad quays that ran along the two sides of the rushing River Rhone. The Lake of Geneva was twinkling with the silver sails of boats that floated across the blue water. On the bridges crossing the river, people, carriages, and motor cars were passing.

An island was in the middle of the river — a little island, covered with shade trees, on which was the statue of a man seated on a high pedestal.

"I wish I could go to that island," Anton said.

As he spoke, a pretty young woman in a brown silk dress who was standing by him, turned and said pleasantly, "That is Rousseau's Island. I am going there now. Will you and your little sister come with me?"

"She is not my sister. She is Trini from Bern," Anton explained shyly. He was a little afraid of the stranger, she seemed so fine in her city clothes.

"Ah, Trini from Bern!" The young woman smiled

kindly down at Trini. "Will you and this young gentleman come to the island with me?"

"He is not a young gentleman. He is Antonli," Trini
said gravely. "We live together in his chalet, with
Sausage and the Traveler." The stranger appeared so
friendly and interested that Trini wanted to tell her
everything about the lovely home among the mountains.

And she did. For the young woman held their hands,
and together they walked over the bridge that led to
Rousseau's Island. As they went, Trini told about Dete,
and their parents, and the dear city, Bern.

"Your chalet in the mountains must be a happy place
indeed!" the stranger said. "And Bern is a lovely old
city. I have often been there."

"Where do you live now?" asked Anton. He was not
shy any longer, for the stranger looked so friendly.

"I am a teacher," she replied. "In the winter I teach
in the Lötschen Valley, far, far away from here."

"Is it like Geneva — your valley? Has it white buildings and parks and fountains, and a river with seven
bridges?" Anton wanted to learn whether there was
another city as fine as Geneva.

The teacher smiled at Antonli's question.

"Antonli," she said, "I wish you could see that valley
and *my* chalet! A cow, two goats, and seven chickens
live in the same house with me. They sleep downstairs
and the woman who owns the chalet, and I, sleep up-
stairs."

Anton laughed.

57

But Trini gasped. "You sleep in the same house with the goats?"

"Do the goats and the cows and the chickens make a noise together?" Anton asked. He was thinking what loud noises the cows and goats made in the shed at home.

"Some nights they do," the young woman said. Then she told them more about the Hidden Valley of Lötschen.

"It is sixteen miles long and surrounded by great mountains, and the only way to enter the valley is through a deep pass."

"O-o-h!" whispered the children.

"There are mighty glaciers, and always in the spring we are afraid lest avalanches of snow and ice and rocks may sweep down the mountain side upon us in the valley. And if that happened, no one outside could help us, for the pass would be filled with high snow. We should be smothered under the avalanches or crushed to death."

"O-o-h," whispered the children. They looked so frightened and excited that the young teacher told them at once about some of the pleasant things in the Lötschenthal.

She told them how the Lötschen women spun and wove cloth for their dresses, and dyed it by boiling with bark from the alder trees or with yellow moss. What odd clothes the Lötschen boys and girls wore! The men, during the long winter days and evenings, carved beautiful wooden things for their homes; and delicious were the cheeses that the valley folk made, which they kept stored away for many years.

"Sometimes when a baby is born," said the teacher, "a big cheese is made and carefully put away. When the child grows up and marries, that same cheese is eaten by him and his friends at his wedding feast. And, Antonli, the fountains in the village are not made of stone like the fountains in Geneva. The valley fountains are logs of wood, hollowed out. The waters flow through them."

By this time they had reached Rousseau's Island. There were shade trees near the statue and a little restaurant in the distance. The strange lady led the children to the statue of Rousseau.

"He was the son of a watchmaker of Geneva," she told them. "He was a man of great learning and wrote famous books which made the people of Geneva proud of him. So they built this statue to honor him."

Anton pointed to the pen which the statue held up in the air, and said, "There is the pen he wrote with!"

Suddenly came a great whirring of wings, and a flock of sea gulls flew up from the water and perched on the railing along the water front.

"Gulls! Gulls!" the children shouted, and ran toward the glistening birds that waited tamely for them. The gulls were used to people and expected to be fed by everyone who visited the island. Trini remembered the roll tucked away in her coat pocket.

"It was for the Traveler," said she, as she broke it into little pieces and scattered them on the ground, "but these gulls look so hungry. If I don't feed them they will grow thin."

Indeed, they did seem starving! With shrill screams and chatterings, the graceful, gleaming birds settled on the ground, and instantly the crumbs disappeared. Then they flocked round Trini, screaming and chattering for more.

"There, they have had their lunch," the teacher said. "Now we shall have ours," and she led the children to the restaurant. They sat outside on small chairs and rested, while they sipped hot, foaming chocolate from tiny cups.

"Come," she said when the little cups were empty, "the father must not wait for you. He might think that the gulls had eaten you both!" And she led them again to the bridge and back to the quay on the river shore.

Then Father Fasel's automobile came chugging down the broad street.

"Here is Vaterli!" Trini started to run to meet him.

"Wait!" laughed the teacher. "Let us shake hands. And, Antonli, if you ever come to my Valley of Lötschen, I shall introduce you to my family, the goats and cows and chickens." She nodded gaily to them both and walked away as the big automobile drew up to the curb.

Trini scrambled into the car and nestled in her seat, talking every minute of the stranger. Anton told Father Fasel at once about the Hidden Valley surrounded by snow-mountains and glaciers, and of the avalanches.

Father Fasel was pleased to hear of their good time. But evening was coming, and he drove in haste out of the city to the road that led up into the hills. Soon they had left the Lake of Geneva far behind.

The sun sank back of the mountains, leaving streaks of red and gold across the clouds. They went up winding, zig-zag roads through thick pine woods. The trees stood like tall black figures. Cows' big bells and goats' little bells sounded from the meadows, *tinkle, tinkle, jingle, jingle, jingle*. Darkness came. The moon rose and hung like a mirror in the blue-black sky, and the stars gleamed and sparkled like diamond points.

Curled up in the back seat of the car, Anton and Trini fell sound asleep. Then the next thing they knew, there they were at home in the brown-eaved chalet.

61

UP–THE–ALP–DAY

THE golden sun shone on the valley in the shadow of the mountains. It was late spring and Up-the-Alp-Day —when the cows of the farms and villages are taken far up into the higher hills to pasture there through the summer.

The family in the Rämis' chalet awoke before sunrise, to see the cows pass up the road. And their own two cows were to join the herd when it reached their hill slope.

From below came the tinkling of many bells. It sounded nearer and nearer.

"They are coming! The cows are coming!" shouted Anton to Trini. He poked his head through the kitchen door and then darted off. Trini hopped down from the bench in the kitchen, where she and Dete sat eating a breakfast of bread and of strawberries as big as pigeon's eggs. She ran out of doors.

Mother Rämi dropped her mop, swung Dete to her back, and called to Mother Fasel, who was washing dishes, "The cows, Mathilde! The cows are here!" And both followed the children down the road.

The herd had reached the village which lay below the Rämis' chalet. How sweet the bells rang! *Tinkle! tinkle! tinkle!* their clear notes echoed over the hills. Then slowly the long procession of cows, with their herdsmen, appeared above the slope and came toward the chalet.

Some of the cows had been brought by train from the towns farther away from the pastures, and had joined the cattle waiting for them. Now they all came together, with bells ringing, leather harnesses shining with brass and dainty carvings, and flowers fastened on their heads and about their necks. The village folk came too, to bid the herdsmen goodbye, for they were to be away in the mountain pastures till autumn.

At the head of the herd came the villagers. How gay they looked! The women and girls wore their old Swiss costumes, with velvet bodices and long embroidered aprons. Their heads were decked with little caps and streaming ribbons. These clothes were kept for holidays.

The men and boys, too, were dressed for the great day.
In velvet and gilt-buttoned vests, short knee-trousers,
and jaunty caps, they ran beside the cattle, swinging
tasseled whips and singing the "Cattle Song."

The cows seemed happier than all. They knew that

soon they would be feeding in delightful places filled with
rich grasses and sweet herbs. At the head of the herd
came the cow-leader. She was a great white and black
animal with short, low-set horns wreathed about with
blue gentian buds and pansies. Her copper bell was

bigger than any other cow's bell. She tossed her posy-crowned head proudly, for she seemed to know that she had taken the prize the year before for being the finest cow in the canton.

The herd stopped before the chalet, and Father Rämi led out his two cows. They, also, were covered with wreaths, and each one had a grand harness of leather that Father Rämi had cut. The harness was studded with little round buttons of brass and fringed with crimson wool tassels.

Trini and Anton proudly watched them join the procession of cows. Then Trini spied Johannli among the crowd. He was standing by some of his own cows, which were to be sent to the pastures for the summer.

Johannli did not look happy. He was not going with the herd. He hated to be parted from his cows. He gripped his ash stick and patted the necks of his favorites, talking to them in a low voice.

"Goodbye, goodbye, Blossom! Goodbye, Golden One! I shall have only the goats to take care of now," he was whispering, and for a minute forgot to scowl.

"Johannli! Oh, Johannli!" Trini called out. He turned and saw her skipping up and down and waving her hands to him. She ran over to where he stood, and said, "Johannli, your cows are the prettiest of all. Look, what lovely flowers they have about their horns!"

That pleased Johannli. He had been up since dawn, gathering primroses and daisies and weaving them into garlands for his pets. He dearly loved the cows that he had guarded for three years. He was sure that Trini meant her praise, and his face lost a little of its crossness, as he answered a bit gruffly:

"This one is called Mother Cheese. Her milk is so rich and yellow that it makes the best cheeses in Switzerland." Then he added, "I am going to own a cheese factory."

"O-o-oh, Johannli!" Trini danced up and down. "When? When will you be a cheese-maker?"

Johannli looked wise and stroked Mother Cheese's heavy neck.

"When I am a man—very soon."

Trini looked happy at this.

"Will you let me visit your cheesery?" she coaxed. "I am going to be here all summer. I have never seen a big cheesery—like the one yours will be."

The cross lines came back to the herdboy's face.

"You will have to wait till mine is built," he snapped.

Trini darted back to her mother.

"Mutterli, Johannli is going to have a cheesery, and I may visit it."

Mother Fasel laughed. She patted Trini's curls.

"The father will take you to visit a cheesery, you and Antonli, and Johannli may go too." She nodded to the tall herdboy, who sulkily followed Trini, whisking his ash stick about.

"Johannli," she asked, "do you want to see a big cheese factory?"

"No!" answered the boy without raising his eyes. He seemed to hate everything except his cows.

Mother Fasel looked surprised. Then she drew Trini away to watch the herdsmen — eight sturdy men — who were getting ready to drive the cattle up the mountain.

The herdsmen were strapping to their own shoulders their leather pouches of salt for the cows. Then one took up the reins of a little cart drawn by a gray mule. In the cart were piled pots and kettles and rolls of bedding and blankets to use up among the hills.

Then the alphorns sounded, first one, then another, till the air rang with the cheery music and echoes.

The wives and daughters of the herdsmen kissed them goodbye. The cattle, tossing their heads, switching their tails, shaking and clanging their bells, were driven into line. Off went the long troop, while the villagers stayed behind, waved their hands, and sang louder than ever.

Over the slope and away to the next village a few miles higher up, went men and cows. *Jingle! tingle! jingle!* called the sweetly-tuned bells. Above the music the village church bell pealed gaily.

In a few moments the procession passed out of sight. The villagers hurried back to their daily tasks. The family at the Rämis' chalet returned to the pretty brown-eaved house on the glistening, flowered hillside, and the air was still ringing with the chimes of those far-off bells and the voices of the herdsmen singing their cow-song and yodeling:

> "The springtime is here,
> The heavens are clear,
> The melted snow's falling,
> The cuckoo is calling,
> For May now is here!
> *A hoa ho, a loa ho,*
> *Ja lo ho, a jo a*
> *Lo a jo a, lo a du a!*"

OFF TO THE CHEESERY

"Hurry, Trini! Antonli, bring the dinner basket!" called Mother Rämi.

All during July the village men had been busy in the hay fields. The meadows in the valleys were cut first, and their hay stored away in the barns. Now the men were climbing up into the higher hills far from the town, to cut the grass and make hay in the pastures there.

But the Rämi family from the chalet were going to visit a cheese factory.

Trini ran out of the chalet. Anton followed. He was dragging a long rush basket covered with a red tablecloth. Both children climbed into the car, where Mother Rämi, with Dete on her lap, and Mother Fasel were waiting.

Father Rämi sat in the front seat with Father Fasel, who was to drive the automobile to the old town on the shores of the Lake of Geneva, where the cheese factory stood.

They drove slowly down the mountain side into the valley. Anton and Trini sat listening to the fathers, who were talking about the splendid roads in the valleys, which the Swiss government took such pains to keep in order, and of the lakes and rivers whose water-power was being used to run the electric machines in the big chocolate factories. They talked of many things.

The children could not understand all they said, but they knew that the men in the Swiss government were doing splendid things for Switzerland. Trini was proud that her father worked for the government.

"Yes, yes," Father Rämi was saying, "our kitchen salt and the salt we feed the cows is got from the salt pits in the canton of Vaud."

Suddenly the car stopped and Father Fasel jumped out to examine a broken spot in the road, where a heavy rock had fallen from an overhanging crag. It had dropped in the roadway, breaking the smooth ground.

The children scrambled out too, for they saw a cherry tree growing in a little orchard close to the road.

The tree was thick with shining leaves, and the cherries hung, like crimson rubies, on little pale green stems among the branches.

"The tree is so full of cherries! Perhaps we can get some!" Anton said. He picked up a handful of little stones and threw them into the lower branches.

"Antonli!" It was his mother's voice. "Those cherries don't belong to you."

"Anton!" It was his father's voice. "Drop that stone."

Anton turned. Then across the field came the farmer himself, shaking a rake.

"What is this, young man?" he scolded. "Have you not been taught in school that the berries and fruit in Switzerland are too precious to be wasted? As for stealing—bah!"

"But," exclaimed Trini, "they are not going to be wasted. We shall eat them. I will carry them in my hood, so." She held out her pink hood.

The farmer looked down at her, then laughed suddenly.

"You are a cherry blossom yourself," said he. "But these cherries are mine, and I will give *you* some." He drew down a branch and filled the hood.

Then he turned to Anton.

"What do they teach you in school about our fruits?" he thundered.

Anton looked ashamed. He dropped the stones on the ground but answered bravely, "Never to destroy them." Then he added, "I did not mean to hurt the tree. I did not think you would care if I took a few. The birds are eating them."

The farmer saw that the boy was sorry and nodded to the mothers in the car, saying kindly, "Well! well! If those birds are taking a breakfast from my tree, you may have a few bites too." And he broke off a small spray laden with fat red fruit and held it out to him.

"Thank you, sir!" Anton's eyes shone as he took the cherry branch. He ran back to the car where Trini sat, the hood in her lap, admiring her cherries.

Of course the fathers scolded. The mothers explained that it was wrong to take anything that belonged to another. Then the children settled soberly down and commenced to nibble the sweet, juicy cherries, while Father Fasel drove on.

Before midday everyone was hungry. The automobile was drawn up by the roadside, and the family sat on the grass, to picnic under the shade of a great chestnut tree. There the basket was unpacked.

Thick slices of cheese, boiled eggs, whole-wheat bread covered with delicious butter, cold boiled potatoes sprinkled with salt, wild-strawberry jam in a little cup, and milk chocolate, each kind of food wrapped in a napkin by itself, all were spread out on the grass.

Everybody talked, and everybody ate till there was nothing left except the cup and the napkins.

"It is time to start," Father Fasel said at last. "We shall reach the factory in an hour." And away they drove toward the Lake of Geneva, which they could see sparkling in the distance.

At last they drove into the town which nestled on the lake shore, with snow-capped mountains looking down on the blue water and the town. They went at once to the cheese factory.

THE HOUSE WHERE CHEESE WAS MADE

"Antonli, look!" Trini pointed to a pretty young woman in a brown silk dress who stood in the hall of the cheese factory. She was watching a workman pushing a wheelcart stacked with cheese loaves. These cheeses had been taken from the press and were going to the cellar to have a salt bath.

The fathers had wandered off to the packing room to see cured cheeses put into barrel-like tubs. They were to be sent on by railroad to France, and from there they would be shipped to America.

The mothers had left little Dete asleep in the automobile and stood in the hall talking to the cheese-maker.

74

He was saying that he had ordered from some of the farmers of the district all their cows' milk for six months, and he had leased their cheese factory with its fine electric-running machines.

Anton and Trini were going in and out of the large, clean rooms that opened from the hall, when they spied the stranger in the brown silk dress.

She turned when Trini spoke, and the children knew her at once. She was the pretty young teacher who lived in the Hidden Valley.

"Antonli! Trini!" The teacher, smiling with delight, held out her hands and came toward them. "What are you doing here?"

"We are visiting this cheesery," said Anton.

"And Mutterli is here too." Trini caught the teacher's hands and pointed to where the mothers were talking at the other end of the hall.

"Come," said the teacher, "let us hear what the cheese-maker says." And she went with the children and stood by Mother Rämi and Mother Fasel.

The cheese-maker was saying, "The boys bring in the milk from the farms twice a day. We weigh the milk on those scales there, so we know just how much milk each farmer's cows give."

Anton listened, but Trini did not take her eyes from the pretty teacher. She had no ears to hear about milk or cheese just then.

"Mutterli," she whispered, "the teacher from the Valley of Lötschen is here."

How pleased the mothers were to meet her! The
teacher told them that she was visiting all the factories
in that district. She said her name was Regina Barrelet,
and her home city was Neuchâtel.

"Come with us," begged Mother Fasel. "We are
going down to the storage cellar, where the cheeses are
kept till they are sent out to the markets."

The cellar was dimly lighted. The children had never
seen so many cheeses before. Great, round, pale, creamy
cheeses and huge wheels of butter-yellow cheeses, some
weighing over two hundred pounds, were stacked in rows
on shelves all round the walls of the room.

The cheese-maker pointed to the loaves of lovely pale cheeses and said, "This cheese was made in winter, when the cows eat dry hay and beet-roots and the milk is not rich — and this — " he touched a butter-yellow wheel on another shelf, "was made in summer, when the cows feed on rich herbs and grasses." He was proud of his fine Gruyère cheeses and loved to tell everybody just how they were made.

Anton looked on in amazement. He thought of the little cheesery near his chalet. He was glad that he did not have to scrub the shelves in *this* cellar! The niches in the wall of his own cheesery, where Father Rämi kept the cured cheeses, were easy to scour; but if he had to wash down all these shelves it would take him a year.

Then they returned to the large, clean room above, where the milk curds, looking like beautiful, thick snow, were warming in a big copper kettle over an electric fire. Just then a workman came with a wooden shovel and cut the curds, which had changed to a jelly-like mass, into little pieces.

Anton and Trini watched him work for a long time. Then they saw him lift the curds out of the kettle in a big cloth attached to a rail which was fastened to the ceiling. Then the cloth full of curds was carried over to a table to be put under the press.

"Tomorrow this pressed cheese will have a salt bath in the salt cellar," said the workman, nodding to the children, who stood looking on.

"I know," said Anton.   He told the workman how he helped his father make the cheese at home.

But Trini did not know; so she asked, "Then what will it do?"

"After it has lain in its salt bath for two weeks, it will take a long rest for six or eight weeks in a nice warm cellar.   While it is there it will ferment and ripen, and a thick rind will form round it.   It will grow delicious, smooth, and rich."

"Then what will it do?"

"It will be weighed and tapped to find out how heavy it is and whether it is well made," answered the workman.

Trini was going to ask what would happen next, but the workman told her at once.   "Then it will go down to the storage cellar and stay on a shelf till it is sent out into the world to be eaten by boys and girls, perhaps in England, or in France, or in America."

Trini was wishing that she had a piece to eat at once, when Father Rämi came to the door and called, "Come, all of you, it is time to go home.   Dete is awake."

The mothers and the teacher had become good friends. When the hour arrived for the family to go home, Mother Rämi begged her to drive with them and visit the chalet.

Regina shook her head.   "No, no, I cannot go today. But before school opens in September, I will visit you."

Everyone went outside the factory.   The children were surprised to discover that it was sunset time.   The evening milk was being brought in.   Big boys, with long wooden pails of it strapped to their shoulders, were

78

coming up the road. Some of the farmers had sent their milk in great cans, piled in wooden carts dragged by dogs. By each dog-cart a boy walked, waving a tasseled whip or a slim stick. The dogs had little jingly bells tied about their necks, and the boys were whistling and singing.

"This milk will make more of your tasty cheese," said Regina, as the boys and carts stopped before the factory door.

And while the car drove away, she waved her handkerchief and called out, "Anton! Trini! I shall go in September to see the Traveler and Sausage."

Then she vanished altogether, for Father Fasel drove fast out of the town, back to the chalet on the mountain slope.

HAY–SUNDAY FESTIVAL

ANTON and Trini stood on the slope, waiting for the mothers.

It was the Hay-Sunday Festival. That great day comes in the middle of August, when the people of the nearby villages celebrate together the harvest time.

All the hay had been gathered in from the lower meadows. The men and boys had been busy for several weeks in the upper pastures, cutting and hauling the hay down to the barns. The work was hard, for those high mountain pastures could not be reached by reaping machines or carts. All the work had to be done by hand. The men and boys had mowed the grass by hand, and packed the dried hay into big burlap sheets, which they had carried down the mountain sides on their backs.

Now the Hay Festival was here! How happy were Anton and Trini!

The jolly festival was to be held in a meadow near the Rämis' chalet. This field made a good place for merrymaking. It was very large and was covered with short grass and starry red and blue gentian flowers. All along one side stood pine and fir trees. And behind the meadow rose a high rock, where great beds of rose-colored rhododendrons grew down to the meadow's edge.

Anton and Trini, while waiting for their mothers, jumped about on the slope near the cheesery, so eager were they to start. Trini was dressed in a little Bernese festival dress, made like the clothes which Bernese women wore long ago.

She looked like a little dwarf-woman. She wore a snow-white waist with puffed-out sleeves reaching to her elbows. Her skirt was red and very long, and her black velvet bodice, laced with bright ribbons, was dotted down the front with tiny rosettes like open flowers. A cap with wide frills stood out about her curls like the wings of a big butterfly. And she was wearing the wooden shoes that Father Fly Eyes had given her.

Anton had on his Easter suit and leather shoes. He carried an alpenstock decorated with crimson rhododendrons, while in his straw hat he had stuck a bunch of the same flowers.

Just then Mother Rämi came out of the chalet.

"Come, come!" called Trini. "We shall be late."

"Mutterli, they have the Swiss flag!" shouted Anton. "I see it waving from the pole, all red with the big white cross!"

"Hurry along," answered Mother Rämi, as she picked up Dete to carry her on her hip.

The children sprang down the hill like little chamois. Trini's stiff skirt stood out like a balloon as she ran. She had a hard time to keep the wooden shoes on her feet, but they looked so fine with her Bernese dress that she would not take them off. So Anton was bounding far ahead when she reached the meadow. He laughed teasingly as she came running up and dropped breathless on the grass. He sat down beside her.

"These wooden shoes," she panted, "were made for a great lady in a palace."

"Pooh!" answered Anton scornfully. "Grand ladies wear shining shoes." His own feet were hurting in their high leather boots. He stretched them out before him and shook his head as he added, "I think that bare feet are the best shoes. They never squeeze or pinch. When I am a man, I shall always go barefoot."

Trini opened her eyes very wide.

"Anton! My father always wears shoes and so does yours," she exclaimed. "You will have to wear shoes."

"Only on Christmas and New Year's and Easter Day!" Anton's voice was firm. He knew that his feet could never get used to being pinched by hard leather.

"You will have to wear shoes when you are a man," said Trini firmly; but she added softly, "When you visit me at Bern, you may take off your shoes and go barefoot, and so will I!"

Just then the two mothers came and called them. The children, forgetting their stiff feet, ran off toward the crowd that had gathered near the flag, which was hoisted on a tall larch pole in the middle of the meadow.

All the folk from the villages stood in a circle. Women and girls were dressed in the quaint old Swiss costumes that their grandmothers had worn and that were put on now only for festivals. The pretty dresses made the crowd bright with gay beribboned aprons and glistening bodices. Some of the mothers held spick-and-span babies in their arms. Their slips, newly washed and starched, stood out like petals on a rose.

The boys raced up and down and waved tiny Swiss

flags and long alpenstocks wreathed about with leaves and crimson rhododendrons. Everyone was laughing and talking. Mother Rämi and Mother Fasel joined a group of women who had known Mother Fasel when she was a girl and lived in the village.

Anton darted away and followed the shouting boys. Trini wanted to race with them, but all the other little girls were standing quietly by their mothers in the circle, and she was ashamed to play like a boy. She was wondering what to do, when she spied Father Fly Eyes among a group of men. Trini ran over and stood quietly by his side. She hoped he would notice her wooden shoes.

He did. He saw the wee wooden gentian-buds peeping from the folds of Trini's skirt, and knew them at once.

"Well, well, little Wise One!" the wood-carver exclaimed. "You have the prettiest feet! Those shoes are fit for a grand lady in a palace."

Trini held out one foot and waved it up and down.

"Palace ladies wear shining shoes," she said, "and they pinch and squeeze."

The old man laughed.

"No shining shoes can be so fine as your wooden ones. Yours are made of our splendid chestnut wood," he said.

Suddenly an old herdsman with a bushy white beard, and wrapped in a long black cape, stepped slowly and gravely into the circle. He carried a huge, curved wooden alphorn, longer than himself, and on this he blew a few notes.

"Hush!" said Father Fly Eyes. He took Trini's hand, and both were silent as the sweet, clear notes rang over the meadow. All in the circle stood quiet, while that lovely music, which meant "Praise ye the Lord," was played by the old herdsman.

When the alphorn was silent, there was a bubbling of gay voices, while a dozen girls from a village higher up on the mountain stole out on to the green meadow. They were all wearing the native costume of the women of a far-off canton, where their mothers had lived before they came to live in the region of Gruyères.

Each girl wore a long, full skirt with an apron bordered with strips of colored ribbons. Each one had a velvet bodice and waist with snowy white sleeves. On each head was a cap with lace-like butterfly wings. The girls carried milk pails, which they swung back and forth as they sang this cattle song:

> "In the happy springtime,
>   When the alp awakes,
>   See! on the mountains —
>   *Ohe*, for the milk pails!
>   *Ohe*, for the milk pails!
>   Herdsmen are climbing;
>   Cowboys are climbing;
>   Sunday clothes they're wearing;
>   On their hats are flowerets;
>   Vests with little sleevelets,
>   Big bells and little bells!
>   *Ohe! Ohe!*
>   Salt in 'broidered leather
>   On the green alp!
>   In the pretty meadow!
>   There go the herdsmen,
>   There go the herdsmen.
>
> "In the happy summer,
>   When the alp is fresh,

The pretty herdsmen—
   Ohe! on the mountain—
   On the peak!
With the merry singing,
Do all their duties;
Drink from the snow-streams,
Lead to the pasture
The happy cows;
Make all the milk-food.
   Ohe! Ohe!
The cheese and the butter!
   On the green alp,
   In the pretty meadow!
There go the herdsmen,
There go the herdsmen!

"In the mid-summer,
When the alp is ripe,
Watch all the herdsmen—
   Ohe! with the
Sun on the flowery fields,
Hold a feast together;
Dancing the round dance;
Singing, leaping, shouting,
Dancing, yodeling, whistling!
Kissing their maidens!
And the alpine pasture,
Buzzes like a beehive—
   Ohe! Ohe!

When the bees are free!
On the green alp,
In the pretty meadow!
There go the herdsmen,
There go the herdsmen!" *

There was a clapping of hands when the song was over and a buzz of praise sounded from all sides. The

* Translated by permission of the publishers, Jobin & Cie, Lausanne (Switzerland). All rights reserved.

happy girls blushed with joy and ran back into the circle.

Then cheery music followed. The herdsmen played their mouth-organs, the shepherds yodeled, the children piped gay little tunes they had learned in school; and above all these sounds was heard the clear, ringing note of the great alphorn.

When the wrestling came, everyone was still. Anton and the other boys pushed their way to the front of the crowd, and with shining eyes watched the young village men give a grand display of their strength and skill, throwing one another on the grass.

The afternoon passed so quickly with singing, dancing, and sports that it seemed but a few minutes long, when Anton and Trini heard the church bell ring. It was sunset, and the Hay Festival was over.

With light talk and laughter, the mothers called together their children, bade one another goodbye, and lugged the sleepy babies across the meadows or up the mountain side to their homes. Some of the men stayed behind to talk of the harvest, their cheese-making, and the things the farmers were doing that summer.

Mother Fasel held Dete, while Mother Rämi went in search of Anton and Trini. She called, "Supper! Trini! Anton!" several times before Anton, who was turning somersaults on the grass with the other boys, came rolling toward her like a cart wheel.

"I am just learning to do what the wrestlers did," he grumbled. "Why do we have to go so soon?"

"Stand up!" said his mother severely. "You can learn tomorrow." Then she turned away to find Trini.

Trini still sat by Father Fly Eyes. She held the wooden shoes in her lap, while she listened to a story the old wood-carver was telling. She stood up when Mother Rämi called and said mournfully, "I am listening to a story. Why do we have to go home so soon?"

"You can hear it another time," rebuked Mother Rämi. Then she greeted the old wood-carver.

Father Fly Eyes had known Mother Rämi since she was a little girl. He was delighted to talk to anyone, for he seldom left his hut on the high mountain side.

Mother Rämi asked him kindly if he had many sales for his carved pieces. And, as she bade him goodnight, she added, "You must come down to our house for supper when Regina Barrelet comes." And she told him all about the young teacher.

Trini's face brightened at that. She stroked the old man's hands and coaxed him to come soon.

"You can tell me the end of that story," she whispered.

"Yes, yes!" the old man nodded. "I shall come, and you shall hear everything that happened."

Then over the meadow and up the hill the mothers went with sleepy little Dete. Anton and Trini trudged slowly behind them. Anton was rubbing the bruises on his shins, which he had got in wrestling with the boys. Trini carried both wooden shoes under her arms.

Hay-Sunday Festival was over! Bare feet, supper, and bed — those seemed very good!

WHAT WAS IN THAT BAG?

THE early September wind was blowing hard. Old
Father Fly Eyes trudged down the pass with his alpen-
stock in one hand and a bag strapped to his shoulders.
He was going to the chalet to have supper with Mother
Rämi's family.

91

The night air was cold and stinging. The pine trees shook their needles like tinkling icicles. Fallen leaves from the chestnut trees scurried and whirled along the ground, as though they were wee, dancing, brown elves.

Father Fly Eyes pulled down his old felt hat and drew his cloak close.

"Autumn is come," he said to himself. "Soon winter will be here." And he walked more quickly toward the light flickering from the chalet's window in the valley below.

When he reached the house, it was Anton who saw him first. He was standing by the window staring out at the distant mountains, which loomed so high, so still, so near the stars. Then Anton saw the old wood-carver.

"Here he is, Trini!" he shouted, and darted forward to open the kitchen door.

Trini sat in the room next the kitchen. This room was never used by the Rämis except when there was company.

In the spring, when Mother Rämi cleaned the house, this guest room was scrubbed all over, wooden walls, wooden floor, and all the heavy wooden furniture. She hung curtains freshly starched and ironed at the two square windows and then closed the door. The family never went into that shining place, unless a guest arrived.

Now Regina Barrelet had come, and she and Trini were sitting in the big guest room, on a bench beneath the cuckoo clock hanging on the wall. This clock did not tell the time like the one in the kitchen, for it was never

92

wound. The room looked very cosy, for Mother Rämi had lighted a fire in the great stove and had brought from the kitchen her pots of bright flowering geraniums for the windowsills, all in honor of the young teacher's visit to the chalet.

When Trini heard Anton call, "Here he is!" she jumped from the bench and ran into the kitchen. Mother Rämi and Mother Fasel were greeting the old wood-carver. They took off his heavy cloak and hat and hung them on a peg back of the door. Father Fly Eyes unstrapped his bag and stood it in one corner.

"There are my children, in here," said he, tapping the bag.

"Your children?" Trini poked the bag to see if it held anything alive. "What kind of children have you?" she asked.

"There's a baby chamois in it!" guessed Anton. He knelt down and felt all over it. But it was hard and knobby and stuck out in sharp points and edges. "He is all bones, this chamois," said Anton, shaking his head.

"If a chamois were in that bag," laughed Father Fly Eyes, "he would make a whistling noise. That is what little chamois do when they are frightened. Wait! After supper I will show you my children."

Then Regina came into the kitchen to see what was happening. Soon everyone was sitting around the supper table and talking.

Mother Rämi had prepared piping hot sausages, creamy bean soup, fresh whole-wheat bread, golden butter, boiled lamb, and rich toasted cheese chunks. Mother Fasel had baked gingerbread bears, like the kind sold in the bakers' shops of Bern.

"Ah!" sighed Regina, "I do not have such suppers in my valley."

"I do not have such a princely meal in my hut," exclaimed old Father Fly Eyes. "I would have to sell many wooden carvings to be able to buy a fine dinner like this."

And Anton and Trini nibbled gingerbread bears with their soup and sausages and boiled lamb.

When the supper was over, the family sat near the great stove. Mother Rämi knitted. She was making woolen mittens for Anton. Mother Fasel held Dete in her arms and crocheted a red woolen jacket for Trini to wear at school in winter time. Father Rämi, by the table, cut and carved harness for the cattle from great pieces of brown leather; while Father Fasel was drawing a map of the roads in the canton of Fribourg.

Regina sat on the floor by the stove, with the children curled up at her side.

"Now," said Father Fly Eyes," I shall open my bag and show my children. I am carrying them to the city to sell them!"

He brought the bag from the corner. Carefully he drew out the delicate carved pieces he had carried down from his hut. One by one he laid the little wooden figures on the floor in a long row for all to see.

Such pretty, exquisitely carved wooden things they were! Little chalets with tiny balconies, tiny stairs, tiny windows, and tiny sloping shingled roofs; picture frames with starry edelweiss trailing round their borders; wee men with hoes and rakes; little women holding milk pails; geese with swaying necks; and bears. So many bears there were—bears eating supper, mother bears holding baby bears, dancing bears, and bears sitting beneath big umbrellas! And each wooden piece was so lightly and daintily cut and carved that it seemed to belong to a fairy world.

"O-oh!" whistled Anton.

"O-oh!" sighed Trini.

"How beautiful! How clever!" cried Regina.

The fathers and mothers smiled and nodded. They were pleased that their old friend's handiwork was so admired.

"How did you ever learn to do such wonderful work?" Regina asked. She held up a little figure of a herdsman with a lively goat skipping by his side.

"I was born in Brienz," the old man answered proudly.

Trini started up and caught his hand, crying out, "Brienz! That is the city you were telling me about at the Hay-Sunday-Festival. Please, please finish the story!"

Father Fly Eyes smiled. He moved closer to the fire and said, "Now I'll tell it all over again!"

"Do! Do!" everyone cried.

THE WOODEN VILLAGE

THIS is the story that Father Fly Eyes told:

Once upon a time — and this is a true story — once upon a time a baby boy was born in Brienz. Brienz, you know, is called the Wooden Village, because so many wood-carvers live there. What a pretty Wooden Village it was when that baby boy was born!

It lies at the end of a twinkling lake, and behind it stand tall, fir-clad mountains. The streets of the village are narrow, and its wooden houses have pear and apricot trees climbing over their doors and on their walls. They grow like vines, these fruit trees, and how tempting they look in the summer time, when the golden-pink apricots and yellow pears hang richly among the green leaves.

In this Wooden Village that baby boy was born and he was named Joseph Guttrun. He was the son of a poor wood-carver.

When Joseph grew older, his father taught him to carve. At first he showed him how to hold the sharp tools and taught him to cut simple little flowers and leaves on covers of boxes, which he sold in the shops. As Joseph's hands and eyes became more skilled, his father taught him to carve small figures of the men and women of Brienz, figures of our mountain eagles, and of goats and wild chamois.

One morning, when Joseph was ten years old, he was sitting on the shore of the lake. He was carving an especially fine box. On it was the picture of the Wooden Village, with the lake lying beside it, and the great mountain looking down on the little town.

Just then a man passed by. He stopped when he saw Joseph and examined the carved box, and said, "This is a fine box. If you will let me take it, I will sell it and bring you the money. Where do you live?"

Joseph told him, and the stranger went away with the box.

The next day the stranger came to Joseph's chalet in the Wooden Village.

"I have sold your box to the President's wife in

Lucerne," said he. "Here is your money." And he gave Joseph ten francs.

There was joy in the little chalet. Joseph danced with happiness. Joseph's father told the stranger that he had worked for twenty years, but had never been paid so much money for any one piece of carving. And Joseph's mother cried and kissed the francs, and said that now they would have enough money to buy bread for a week.

"That is good!" answered the stranger. "But I have something to say. Your little Joseph has a fine talent for carving in wood. If you wish, I will take him to my shop and teach him. All the pieces that he makes I will sell, and you shall have the money."

That stranger was Christian Fischer, the great wood-carver of Brienz!

In Christian Fischer's wood-carving shop, little Joseph learned to cut and carve beautifully. It was there he learned to make the little shingled chalets, and the dancing bears, and wee women and men, like the figures I showed you tonight. All that work Christian Fischer sold in the Swiss towns, and Joseph carried the money home every Sunday to his parents.

Years passed, and the father and mother died. Joseph left the little chalet with apricot trees trailing over its door. He left the Wooden Village forever and traveled all the way to the canton of Fribourg.

There among the hills he built a small brown hut, and there he lives today, carving wooden figures as he learned to carve them in the shop of the great Christian Fischer. Almost everybody has forgotten that his name is Joseph. And because the old man — for he is very old now — has such strong, clear eyes, they call him Father Fly Eyes.

And Father Fly Eyes ended his story.

"*You* are that Joseph!" Trini cried.

The wood-carver nodded.

"I will be a wood-carver too," said Anton thoughtfully. He was thinking of what a fine, strong box he would make with his chalet and cheesery and cattle shed carved upon it.

Father Fly Eyes turned and looked at him sharply.

"Go to Brienz, Antonli!" he exclaimed. "Go to the Wooden Village! There is a school in Brienz now, where boys are taught to become wonderful artists in carving wooden things. There are teachers too, who will show you how to draw designs from pictures in art books and from living things.

"And the teachers will take you to the zoo in the Wooden Village," went on Father Fly Eyes, "to watch and study the animals and birds that live there. You will cut out their figures so cleverly that they will look like the wild creatures living in our Swiss mountains and valleys. Go to Brienz!"

Cuckoo! cuckoo! cuckoo! The wooden cuckoo bird in the clock on the kitchen wall poked its head out of its wee swinging door and called *cuckoo* nine times. *Jingle, jingle, jingle,* nine times the tiny bells in the clock chimed out.

99

What a bustle there was! Anton and Trini were hurried off to their beds at once. Father Fly Eyes began to pack away his wooden pieces in the bag, to carry them back to his hut.

In a short time the lights were out, and the family in the brown chalet were asleep.

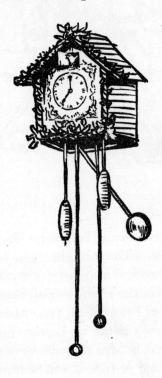

THE DOG–HEADED ALPENSTOCK

IT WAS the afternoon following Father Fly Eyes'
visit to the chalet. The sunlight shone like gold on the
brown shingled eaves. The pine trees stirred and crackled
their stiff needles in the fresh autumn breeze.

"Trini," Mother Fasel called, "you have only five days
more before we go home to Bern. You still have a
yard of lace to crochet for the pillows in your bedroom.
Work fast now, and perhaps it will be finished by supper
time."

So Trini sat on the bench in the sunshine and crocheted
the fine white thread into tiny loops and flowers, wishing

that she could play about with Anton. But Anton ran into the kitchen and came back with a walnut stick in his hand. He sat down by her and began to carve.

"This will be as fine as any alpenstock made by the folk of Brienz," he said proudly.

Trini glanced at him sidewise. She would not let Anton see her look. Oh, no, she felt so cross! What a splendid bear's head he was carving! Such a long nose, such stiff ears, such big round eyes! Anton worked and worked. Last of all he cut with the point of his knife curly little marks all over its head, like the hair that Father Fly Eyes had carved on his wooden Lion of Lucerne.

Trini sat still on the bench. And her lace? Every time she put in the hooked needle, the thread slipped. She had done scarcely three inches. Her little face was puckered with frowns, and she never raised her head.

"There! Look at my alpenstock," cried Anton, holding it out to her. "Do you think that Father Fly Eyes will say I am a good wood-carver?" he asked proudly. His eyes shone, and he waited to see her surprise.

Trini slipped slowly from the bench and looked at the carved head.

"What is it?" she asked. "It looks like one of the dogs that draw the milk carts at home."

"A dog!" Anton scowled.

He snatched the alpenstock back, then turned away and answered, "I thought *you* knew a bear. You live in Bern!"

"A bear!" piped Trini. "But the bears in the bears' den at home do not look like that thing. Yours is a dog!"

She climbed on the bench again, her face puckered into frowns. There they waited in silence. Anton swung his precious alpenstock, Trini swung her bare feet to and fro.

Then she began to hum, "Boys are rude! Boys are rude!"

"Bah!" Anton turned his head and glared at her.

"Girls are stupid! As stupid as bears!" he mocked.

Just then Regina came and stood in the doorway of the chalet. She looked at the two angry children and nodded her head wisely.

"Antonli! Trini!" she exclaimed. "There is a storm in the air! A terrible storm! I feel something dreadful near our chalet. Perhaps it is a glacier, or an avalanche first creeping, then rushing, down our mountain side, or maybe a frightful lightning storm."

Both the children turned at once and looked first at her with amazed eyes, then up into the clear skies, where the golden autumn sunshine shone down on the peaceful mountain slope.

"An avalanche!" cried Anton. "They come when the snow melts in spring. This is September!"

"A glacier!" said Trini scornfully. "I am not afraid! But lightning?" and she jumped quickly off the bench and stood by the young teacher. "Not lightning!"

Regina laughed. "But," said she, "it is not only a snowslide that destroys, or a lightning storm; there are tempests that spoil our happy times. One of them is near now!"

"What?" Anton asked. He had heard his father tell of escaping from the path of fearful avalanches, and of being lost on vast glaciers cut by deep crevasses in the ice. He himself had seen the great storms gather suddenly over the mountain peaks and sweep the valleys with streams of water and sheets of living flame. He did not know of anything else that could be so fearful as they.

He came close to Regina and looked anxiously in her

face. The young teacher drew him to her side and sat on the bench with Trini in her lap.

"Frowns!" said she. "Scowls! Hateful words! Those are the terrible things I feel about our chalet."

The children looked ashamed. Trini picked up her lace to finish it. Anton held up his alpenstock.

"It is a bear," he muttered. "*She*," pointing to Trini, "said it was a dog."

Regina took the crudely carved alpenstock in her hand.

"My brother used to carve in wood, before he became a watch-maker," she said thoughtfully. "And his first figures were very poor indeed. Yours is a little better. But you will have to study, Antonli, and work hard to make even one perfect piece. Father Fly Eyes spent many years in Christian Fischer's shop, you know. Oh, yes, it takes many years to learn anything well," she explained, nodding at Anton as she gave him his stick. "Brother Franzli worked a long, long time before he became a good watch-maker," she added.

Anton looked at his alpenstock. Perhaps Trini was right. Perhaps it was a dog's head, and not the head of a bear that he had carved. He was glad to know that Regina's brother Franzli had carved poor figures too.

"How many years did Franzli work?" Trini coaxed.

Regina glanced sharply over the mountains and up into the cloudless sky, then looked down at the children, and said, "Well, there are no avalanches, nor scowls, nor cross words, about our chalet just now! So I shall tell you of my brother Franzli."

105

FRANZLI, JEWELS, AND WATCHES

THIS is Regina's story:

Franzli and I lived with our grandfather in the town of Neuchâtel. Our parents had died when Franzli was ten years old, and I was only a baby.

Grandfather lived near the lake, and from the balcony of our simple wooden house we could see the vine-clad shore of Lake Neuchâtel and the stretch of pale green waters, with little trading vessels and passenger steamers floating like great birds over the waves.

Grandfather was a furniture-maker. He had a workshop in the center of the town. There he made benches and chairs and wooden tables. It was lovely furniture that Grandfather made, for he carved on them fine figures of flowers and birds and sometimes verses from the Bible.

As brother Franzli grew older, Grandfather taught him to carve in wood and to make simple chairs and stools and posts for beds. But Franzli did not wish to be a furniture-maker. He loved watches. He knew that wonderful things could be made from a piece of wood, but the delicate coiled spring of a watch, its tiny screws, its bits of hard jewels — sapphires, emeralds, or rubies — the thread-like pivots, all the hundred wee pieces that make up a watch, charmed him. He knew that he would never be happy unless he were a watch-maker.

Day after day Franzli stole off from the workshop and went to the watch factory. How he loved to see the workmen running the marvelous machines that turned and cut screws hardly larger than a grain of sand! At other machines he saw skilled men drawing out the delicate wire for watch springs or sawing the teeth on the wee watch wheels.

The men in the factory liked Franzli. He appeared so interested in their work, and often they showed him how to control the machines, and how to put together by hand the hundreds of tiny parts to make a finished watch.

Yes, Grandfather punished Franzli each time he left the workshop. He scolded and stormed, and he boxed Franzli's ears whenever he found Brother's wooden pieces unfinished on the bench.

Now Grandfather owned a handsome watch, which was the delight of his heart. He wore it on his vest all day, and at night he tucked it carefully beneath his pillow. He never wanted it far from him.

One day, when he was putting wooden pegs into the leg of a table, his watch fell from his pocket to the floor. *Whiz-z-z.* The mainspring gave a long, buzzing noise, and the watch stopped running.

"Give it to me, Grandfather," cried Franzli. "I will mend it."

"*You* mend a watch?" exclaimed Grandfather. He laughed scornfully as he said it. "You cannot even make straight legs for a stool."

But he handed Franzli his watch.

"Take it," said he. "If you mend it, you may go to the watch-making school and learn to be a watch-maker. But if you cannot mend it, you must promise me that you will be a furniture-maker."

"I promise," Franzli answered. "But I shall mend your watch."

He did. Franzli mended that watch so well that it was as strong as ever and kept perfect time.

And Grandfather held to his word. He sent Franzli to Le Locle, where he studied in the famous watch school of that town. Three years Franzli studied and worked till at last he was ready to go into the watch factory, and there he became an expert.

Today he knows how to make many kinds of time-pieces: little watches, big watches, torpedo watches, watches to use in airplanes, alarm clocks, and great clocks for churches and factories.

"Is Le Locle near Bern?" Trini asked.

Regina shook her head. "Le Locle is in the canton of Neuchâtel," she answered.

"Does your Franzli make all his watches by hand?" asked Anton.

"No, indeed!" replied Regina. "Years ago watches were made entirely by hand, every part of them. But today we have factories with marvelous machines which make the tiny wheels and springs and many parts that go to compose a perfect watch. But all these little parts are put together by hand."

She pulled back the sleeve of her gown and showed the children a lovely, tiny gold watch fastened to her wrist.

"My Franzli made me this watch," she said. "It is a very fine one."

Anton and Trini admired the dainty golden thing. Its case was traced with trailing vine leaves, and its stem was shaped like a dove.

"You cannot see the bits of wheels inside," said the young teacher. "But they are there beneath the case, and each wheel is on a pivot that rests on a sapphire, for that stone is so hard that it will not wear away when the pivot turns."

"It is so beautiful! So beautiful!" murmured Trini. She patted the shining golden watch on Regina's wrist and wished that she might see the wheels turning on the glistening sapphires. She peered into the wee glass front and rubbed it gently up and down.

Suddenly the ribbon which held the watch slipped. The clasp unfastened, and the delicate watch fell to the ground.

"Oh, Mutterli!" screamed Trini, running into the kitchen. "It's Franzli's watch. I have broken it! Oh, what shall I do?" and she hid her face in her hands.

Mother Fasel was helping Mother Rämi prepare supper. She stopped her work to examine the watch. "Yes, it is broken," she said soberly, "but perhaps Father Rämi can mend it."

Just then Father Rämi, followed by Regina and Anton, came into the kitchen. Trini darted to him and pressed her face on his sleeve.

"I have broken her watch! I have broken Franzli's watch," she sobbed.

"Do not worry, little girl," said Father Rämi. "You shall soon see the good thing that will happen in our chalet!"

In a twinkling he was sitting at the table. His shirt sleeves were rolled up to his elbows. In his hand was a tiny, sharp tool. On the table near him was a black leather case filled with other tools. Before him the golden watch lay with its case in parts and its back open.

Trini stood by him breathless. How big were Father Rämi's fingers! Yet how daintily they held the wee tweezer with which he turned screws in the watch. Trini drew in her breath for fear something would break and spoil his work.

Nothing broke. Father Rämi worked on. He wore a
magnifying glass, through which he peered carefully
at the spring and wheels of the watch, touching them
with a magnet here and there or with tools from the

leather case. At last he nodded happily and fitted the delicate pieces back into the watch case and pressed the parts of the case together. It was done!

"So-ho!" exclaimed Father Rämi and held the watch against Trini's ear.

Tick, tick, tick, tick. That little golden timepiece was running perfectly. Trini laughed aloud.

"It is as fine as ever," said Regina, as she took it to fasten it to the ribbon again.

"Who taught you to cure broken watches, Vaterli Rämi?" asked Trini, kissing his hand and smoothing his cheeks with gratitude.

"Clever Geneva watch-makers," answered he. "When I was a young man, I worked in a watch factory in Geneva during the winter, for there was nothing to do on the farm. I cannot make perfect watches like Franzli's, but I understand how to put together the delicate parts of a watch, and how to mend them if they are not too badly broken."

"Is there a watch factory in Geneva too?" asked Anton. It seemed to him that the City of Seven Bridges held everything fine in the world.

"Indeed, Geneva is the city where the art of watch-making sprang to life in our Switzerland," replied Father Rämi.

Then Mother Rämi bustled up to the table.

"Do you want to eat watches for supper?" she cried. "If you do not let me set the table, we shall have nothing to eat at all."

Father Rämi packed the scattered tools into the leather case and hurried away. Mother Fasel spread the red cloth and set out the milk bowls and big pottery plates. Mother Rämi at once began to toast cheese chunks on a fork before the fire, while thick slices of bacon sputtered in a pan.

Regina picked up Dete and led Anton and Trini into the guest room to play with the carved wooden ninepins that she had brought for the children.

The little chalet was soon echoing with the sound of rolling balls, tumbling pins, sizzling bacon, and happy laughter.

THE STORY OF CHOCOLATE

"We will have supper ready when you all come home tonight!" called Regina.

The fathers and mothers were starting out to visit friends in a village up among the higher hills.

"You must not worry about anything while you are away," added Regina. "Please, please go and have a fine holiday!"

"I will help Regina keep house," cried Trini proudly.

"I will bring in the wood and make the fire," shouted Anton.

"Goodbye! Goodbye!" merrily cried the fathers and mothers.

When the automobile was climbing up the long road to the higher hills, Regina and the children ran into the chalet.

"Antonli, feed the chickens and make the fire; Trini, wash the breakfast dishes," sang out Regina, as she filled the iron tub for baby Dete's bath. "When we have finished the work, we shall make a cake to surprise the mothers," she called, as Anton bounded out of the door with the basket of grain for the hens.

Soon all the work was done. Anton had lighted a fire in the iron stove in which Mother Rämi did her baking.

The iron stove stood next to the low, square one of soapstone used for heating the kitchen and the living room. The soapstone one was set in the wall so that half of the stove was in the kitchen and the other part in the living room.

Regina bustled about getting together the flour, butter, eggs, and other things for the cake.

"I'll sit here near you and learn how to make a cake," said Trini. She hugged fat Sausage close and curled up in the stove-seat to watch Regina mix the cake dough.

"No!" exclaimed Regina. "No lazy drone can stay in this kitchen. Every one must work. Antonli shall beat the eggs, and you may measure the flour."

Then all three of them made the cake. The golden butter was beaten smoothly into the honey, used instead of sugar to sweeten the cake. The whole-wheat flour was stirred into the creamy milk. Stiff, frothy egg-whites were added, and then spices and soda were mixed into the light dough. The cake was ready to be put into the oven.

"There!" said Regina. She carried a square pan half filled with the dough to the stove. "While our cake is baking, Trini must scrape the chocolate for the frosting."

Regina took down from the shelf a large slab of rich, brown chocolate. Soon Trini, with a knife, was carefully scraping delicate slivers from the big piece.

"It looks just like dirt after the hens have scratched it," said Anton, poking his fingers among the bits of chocolate lying in little heaps on the table.

"Does chocolate grow in the ground?" demanded Trini in surprise. She stopped her work and held up the big slab in one hand. "Did this chocolate grow here, in Switzerland, Regina?"

The young teacher laughed. "That chocolate was *made* in our Switzerland. It does not grow *in* the ground. It grows *out* of it. But not in Switzerland," she answered.

"I know! I know!" said Anton, licking his chocolate-covered fingers in excitement. "I learned about chocolate in school. It grows in red pods on a cacao tree. The pods are full of chocolate beans."

"Yes! Yes!" said Regina nodding. "But where does it grow? Can you tell me that, wise young one?"

"Yes!" answered Anton slowly.

Trini looked at him in amazement. She had not learned about chocolate at her school. She knew only that it was delicious.

"Does the cacao tree, with its long, smooth, shining green leaves and tiny pink flowers, grow in England — in the United States of America — in Germany?" laughed Regina.

Anton shook his head. "The cacao tree grows only in hot lands like South America, Mexico, Ceylon, and — and —— " he could not think of any other country, so he stopped and looked toward Trini to see if she was surprised at his wisdom.

Trini was surprised, and she began to scrape the chocolate again, wishing she knew more about it.

Regina gathered up the chocolate bits and put them into a pan to melt over the fire.

"When the cake is baked, we shall spread this frosting over it," said she. "Then I will show you both something you have never seen."

When the cake — a spicy, chocolate-coated loaf —

stood cooling in the centre of the table, Regina took an envelope from her traveling bag. Anton and Trini watched her open it and draw out a picture.

"What is it?" exclaimed both the children together.

It was the photograph of a big Swiss chocolate factory. It showed the many fine buildings where chocolate is made — chocolate to drink — sweet chocolate to eat — milk chocolate smooth and melting. Clean, splendid houses they were, nestling among tall trees, with a railway track near by, and a train passing over it laden with chocolate made in that very Swiss factory.

"This is only one of our fine factories where chocolate is made to delight the children of the world," said Regina. "See! Here are more pictures."

And the envelope held many other photographs, all pictures of the same chocolate factory. One of them was of the hall where the cacao beans, brought from tropic lands, were being shelled by huge machines. Another showed the light-colored beans being roasted in a metal tank, till they were a rich brown, with exquisite flavor. As Anton and Trini examined each picture, Regina explained the special work of the different machines.

"That machine grinds the beans into powder after they are roasted," said she. "This one mixes the powder with sugar. That one presses and molds the powder into chocolate squares."

Then she told them stories of the discovery of chocolate and of the big modern plantations in far-off lands, where grow the cacao trees. She told them how the cacao pods cling like great, long flower-buds to the trunks and branches.

"Four hundred years ago, when the Spaniards discovered the wonderful empire of the Mexican Indians," said she, "they found the Indians drinking a delicious beverage, rich brown, flavored with vanilla and spices, frothy, and as thick as honey. *Chocolatl* the Indians called it. Their emperor, Montezuma, clad in glowing robes of gorgeous bird feathers, ate his *chocolatl* from golden goblets with a golden spoon. Fifty pitchers full a day he took of the cold, rich, foamy *chocolatl* almost as thick as custard.

"And so chocolate was discovered and introduced to Europe," continued Regina. "Soon factories were established to prepare chocolate for European people to eat and drink. And today, in our Switzerland, we make much of the delicious chocolate that is sold in the markets of the world."

While Anton and Trini listened to the story, the afternoon slipped away and the sun hid itself behind the mountain ranges. The pine trees rustled their crisp needles in the rising wind, and evening shadows crept into the chalet.

At once the pictures were put away. Then the dusky kitchen echoed with the sound of busy feet and busy tongues, the clanking of pans, the clinking of dishes being set on the table, and the crackling of the fire. Supper must be ready for the fathers and mothers when they return from their holiday.

HEROES

Crack, crash, crack! The thunder pealed among the mountains. It was evening. The family sat before the fire in the snug chalet.

R-r-r-r-r-r-r! The mighty thunder roared and rolled from mountain peak to peak. The storm was coming. The wind blew terribly and bent the groaning trees.

120

Heavy clouds gathered over the roof of the chalet. The stars were blotted out. The night was as dark as pitch.

Anton stood at the window. Trini was trembling at his side.

Suddenly lightning flashed and flashed across the heavens. A keen, startling thunder-clap sounded, and the rolling echoes repeated it again and again. Jagged spears of lightning seemed to be striking the mountain side.

"Come away from the window, children," called Mother Fasel.

"Yes, yes!" cried Mother Rämi. "Tell them to come, Vaterli."

"I am not afraid," called Anton.

"The mothers are timid, Antonli," rebuked his father. "Come and sit by the fire, both of you, and hear of the true Swiss heroes who were never afraid."

Trini darted to his side and Anton followed her. The children sat close to Father Rämi, who began his story while the rain fell in torrents on the shingled chalet roof and the mountain-circled valley was swept by the September storm.

"We Swiss are never afraid," said Father Rämi. "The mountains are our fortress. The air of our mountains breathes Freedom. We cherish our independence, and love God and peace.

"Many have been our patriot heroes, some of whom gave their lives for our country. But it was the wonderful archer of Uri, so the Swiss legend says, who was the

121

most romantic hero of them all.   Do you know his story?"

"Yes, yes!" cried Trini.

"Tell it again!" cried Anton.

"To the north of that wonder of modern engineering, the St. Gotthard Tunnel," began Father Rämi, "lies the famous little village of Altdorf. After leaving this tunnel one rides down the mountain through fascinating spiral tunnels with glimpses of beautiful views, like pictures, that one sees only in our Switzerland.   Each view seems lovelier than the last, till one reaches the square of little Altdorf in the canton of Uri. There stands a famous fountain, and near it the giant-like statue of the wonderful archer himself and his noble little son.

"About six hundred years ago a part of our Switzerland was groaning under the tyrannous rule of Austria. Cruel Austrian governors, bailiffs they were called, were sent to rule over us. They oppressed our people and treated them brutally. One of the worst of these bailiffs was Gessler. And how the wicked Gessler was punished, and how the men of Switzerland rose up, I will now tell you.

"Gessler went to Uri and, setting his hat on the top of a pole, he proudly ordered everyone to bow down to it. He who refused to bow was to be severely punished. But William Tell, the archer of Uri, refused to bow to the hat.   Each day, as he passed by the hat on the pole, he held his head high and scorned to look at it.

"This angered wicked Gessler, and he commanded that Tell's young son should be brought to him. Then he

122

stood the child beneath a lime tree in the town square and, placing an apple on his head, he ordered Tell to shoot the apple from the child's head.

"Tell had to do his bidding. He took one arrow and placed it in his quiver. He took another arrow, and praying God that he might save his child, he shot the apple from his brave young son's head. Then he turned to Gessler, crying, 'If that arrow had killed my child I would have shot that other arrow into your heart.'

"Tell fled, and later, for those were terrible times, he shot the tyrant Gessler.

"Then the patriot men of Switzerland, bound by an oath they took at Rütli to defend their land, arose and in time freed our country from the Austrian yoke. William Tell himself is said to have died trying to save a drowning man.

"If you visit Altdorf today," added Father Rämi, "you may see the giant-like bronze statue of the wonderful archer and his boy, and the fountain that stands on the spot where Tell's child bravely faced his father without moving, and let him shoot the apple from his head.

"And if you visit the meadow of Rütli, you will see the spot sacred to all Switzerland, for there our independence was proclaimed. The Swiss government has made Rütli a place of pilgrimage."

The thunder sounded fainter and fainter. The wind blew more gently. The clouds raced above the mountain tops, leaving behind them streaks of sky. The storm was dying.

"I am brave now," exclaimed Trini, "and so is Sausage." She caught up the kitten and held her out for Father Rämi to see. "Look! Sausage is purring. She is not afraid of that awful storm."

Father Rämi nodded. "Yes," he replied, "and there are other Swiss heroes, with four feet! There are those noble beasts who face death in the deep snows to save the lives of friends and foes."

"Yes, yes!" cried Anton. "I know them!"

"They are the St. Bernard dogs, who belong to the good monks on the high Pass of St. Bernard," cried Trini.

Father Rämi nodded. "They are heroes too," he said. "With little first-aid kits tied to them they have sought out many weary travelers fallen in the deep snow and about to freeze to death. But today travel is made easier and safer, and few travelers have to go by way of the St. Bernard Pass.

"Antonli, Trini," said Father Rämi thoughtfully, "remember this. We Swiss cherish independence, but we love God and peace. For centuries past, many people, persecuted and driven from their own countries, have found a safe refuge in Switzerland. And since the Great War, many nations have formed a league to keep the world free from war. The League of Nations has made Geneva its place of meeting. In the League of Nations Palace there, the nations are trying to make a universal peace — 'Peace on Earth, good will to men,' you know," added Father Rämi.

"Oh," exclaimed Trini, "we saw the little Peace children going to school there!"

"Yes, yes," said Father Rämi.

"The storm is over," called Mother Rämi. "We can go to bed."

LEAVES! SKIS!

"Mutterli, may I stay here in Anton's chalet till the cows come down from the pastures?" Trini asked the next day.

She stood on the little stool by the high wooden cupboard, helping Mother Fasel put away the breakfast dishes.

"The cows will not come down till the last of the month. We shall go home to Bern in three days," answered Mother Fasel. "School opens soon, and Vaterli must take you to Lucerne, to the boarding school there."

"I want to see the cheeses that the herdsmen have made in their sheds up in the Alps this summer," said Trini sadly. "Antonli told me that they are round and as big as the wheel of a cart, like the cheeses we saw in the cheesery near the Lake of Geneva."

Trini stood thinking a minute; then she added, "How do the herdsmen carry them down to the village, Mutterli? The mountains are so high, no carts go up there. Do the men bring those big cheeses down on their shoulders?"

Mother Rämi was scouring the top of the long table. She paused when she heard Trini's question, and called out:

126

"What a clacking little tongue you have this morning, Trini! Yes, that is the way they bring the cheeses down to the village now. But it was different when I was a child. Mathilde," she added, smiling, "do you remember how the father took us up to the high pastures when we were children, and how we watched the men roll the cheese-wheels down the highest mountain paths to the carts waiting in the valley below?"

Mother Fasel nodded happily. Indeed, she remembered that far-off day when Mother Rämi's father had taken both little girls high up into the Alps, to the herdsmen's little cabin of pine logs. What a happy morning they had spent playing *cache-cache*, hiding and seeking each other in and out of the hut, under the bed of straw or behind the big copper cheese-kettle! What a fine dinner they had had sitting on the one bench in the little room, drinking delicious fresh milk from tin bowls!

What excitement there was after the meal, when the cheeses were rolled down the slope, like giant wheels, to the waiting carts below in the mountain valley! *Crunch, crunch, crunch!* She could hear now those hard round cheese-loaves spinning over the rocky ground. And how the herdsmen laughed and sang and whistled and yodeled as they ran by their sides. No, indeed, Mother Fasel had not forgotten!

"If Trini goes home in three days," said Anton suddenly, "she will not be here to help us gather in the leaves."

"Late autumn is the time we gather in the leaves, Antonli," said Mother Rämi. "Trini will be at school then, thinking of Christmas."

"What do you do with leaves?" Trini hopped down from the stool and stood close to Mother Rämi.

"Anyone would know you came from the city!" laughed Mother Rämi. "Well, we use leaves for winter bedding for the pigs, cows, and goats. Every autumn the men and boys go up to the forests and bring home on sledges great nets full of fallen leaves. Would you like to sleep on dry leaves?" she asked.

"Oh, yes!" cried Trini, her eyes shining as she thought of the crisp, brown, crackly leaves, and what fun it would be to lie on them.

Anton laughed. "But Trini, you do not have pigs and cows and goats at your home in Bern."

Trini thought a minute, then added proudly, "No, but we have leaves, hundreds and hundreds of them."

"Where?" said Anton. He knew that Bern was a large and lovely city, filled with wonderful old churches, strange fountains, and interesting shops.

"In the great forest which is on the edge of Bern," answered Trini happily. "There are trees, many kinds, and in the autumn their leaves fall. The ground is covered with them. We have enough leaves in our forest to make beds for all the cows in Switzerland."

"Come!" cried Anton. "I will show you something nicer than leaves in our cow shed! Come!" And before Trini could speak, Anton caught her hand and ran with her out of the kitchen and down the slope to the shed.

Anton opened the door and led Trini into the dusky place. There were wooden stalls along the wall for the animals; big rush baskets and round feeding pans stood in corners. On the wall over the stalls was carved in big, trailing letters:

> Healthy cattle and good pasture give heavy cheese and cause rejoicing

"Read that!" exclaimed Anton. "Have you words carved like these in your bedroom at Bern?"

"No," answered Trini at once.

"Our cows are very healthy, for Vaterli keeps them clean and sends them up to the rich pastures in summer and feeds them with fine beet-roots and hay in winter," said Anton proudly.

"Your cheeses are heavy and sweet. That must be the reason," said Trini. Then she pointed to a corner of the shed. "But what are those?"

Standing against one side of the rough wooden wall was a long sledge and above it a high shelf. While Trini was speaking, Anton had dragged from the shelf a pair of wooden skis. They were made from the staves of a barrel, and the straps from strips of leather which Father Rämi had cut while making harness for his cattle.

Trini ran over to examine the skis.

"How lovely they are!" she cried excitedly. "How wonderful to slide down the mountain side over the snow, with those on your feet." She touched the bottom of each ski. "How slippery! What did you shine them with?"

"Candle wax." Anton turned them over and tapped their bases. "Mutterli gave me the candle grease in a cup, and I rubbed them smooth with it. I wish the snow would fall," he said longingly; "then I could ski down the mountain side to school."

"Oh!" Trini's eyes danced. "I wish I could ski to school. But Mutterli makes me go to a boarding school near Lucerne. I live with the other girls in a big château. Each morning we go from the dining room into a study room. We hold our copybooks and walk in line. I wish we might walk through our hall in skis! The teacher won't let us make any noise."

"Pshaw!" exclaimed Anton. "I ski down the mountain side to school with my books in a knapsack and my alpenstock in my hand. I sing and yodel. It is great fun!"

"What do you learn at school?" she asked.

Anton frowned. That was the part of going to school that he did not like. Though he had been going to school since he was six years old, he was sure that books made his head dizzy.

"Reading, writing, arithmetic, geography, history, civics. We study six days of the week, but not on Sunday. We go to church then," he answered. Then he said more cheerfully, "In the early spring, we have nature studies. The teacher takes the classes into the mountains and tells us the way flowers grow and all about the trees."

Trini nodded. "But if you went to school in Bern," she said wisely, "you would learn to speak English." She sat on the edge of the sledge and pulled out bits of hay that had clung between her little bare toes.

"My teachers at the boarding school make us learn English, too, and take us on nature-study trips," Trini added. "This year I am going on long nature-study trips with the older girls. Vaterli has bought me a leather knapsack to carry buns and sweet chocolate in. We have our dinner on the mountains, you know."

"Do you carry an alpenstock?" asked Anton. "It makes climbing the steep mountains safer. All the boys and girls here carry them. We tie flowers to their handles."

132

"I have not any alpenstock." Trini looked at him
mournfully. She wriggled her toes and tucked them
under her skirt as she said sadly, "There are French and
English and American girls in my school. They all
carry alpenstocks."

Anton whistled soberly.   He rubbed his hands across the waxed skis.   Then he said softly, "You may have the one I carved.   The one with the—" He paused, then said bravely, "The one with the *dog's* head on its handle."

"Antonli!   I love it!   I love it!   I want my alpenstock now!"   And swift as an arrow Trini sprang up and flew out of the shed to the house.

Anton put his precious skis on the shelf, closed the heavy door, and followed her.   He was happy that after all Trini liked his first piece of wood carving.

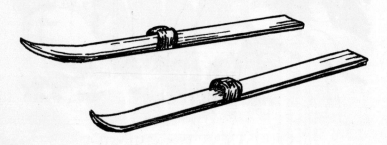

CHRISTMAS IS COMING!

"Whew! It is cold!" Anton, alpenstock in hand, climbed the steep path that led up to the pasture at a distance from the Rämi's chalet. Trini was clambering after with her alpenstock. The children were seeking the goats that had wandered away in search of the spicy thyme which grew among the cliffs.

It was a very cold day for early September. The sky was gray with heavy clouds, and the wind tore and roared through the pines as if it were trying to bring winter before it was due.

Trini nestled into her knitted wool jacket, which she had not worn since the springtime. She was glad that her mother had told her to put on long stockings and boots.

"Those goats are far off," Anton said. "I cannot even hear their bells."

He stood still with raised head and listened. The whistling winds and the rushing in the tree tops, the crisp tinkling of pine needles falling on the dry ground were the only sounds he heard.

"Do you think it will snow today, Antonli?" Trini gasped. She had been clambering fast to keep warm, and the stiff wind had taken her breath.

"I wish it would snow! Then Christmas would soon be here," Anton answered.

"Christmas!" Trini's eyes sparkled. She forgot she was cold. "Vaterli is going to drive to the school near Lucerne and take me home for the holidays. And when I am at home in Bern, Mutterli will show me how to make Christmas cakes. She promised it!"

"What kind of cakes?"

"Bears, and little men and women, baked of ginger-cake dough! They are as big as my two hands." Trini dropped her alpenstock and held up both hands, to show him the size of those gingerbread goodies that her mother baked each holiday time. "They are all covered with pink and white frostings, and they have currant eyes," she said, delighted to watch Anton's own eyes grow big and hungry-looking.

"Can you eat them as soon as they are baked?" he asked.

"No-o-o!" Trini shook her head. "But we pile them on a platter and set them under the Christmas tree. We eat them on Christmas Day."

Then Anton remembered the lost goats. Trini picked up her alpenstock, and they began to climb again. But Anton wanted to hear more about her Christmas tree.

"Are there other things under your tree?" he asked.

"Of course," said Trini. "It is a Christmas tree! There are presents for all of us, wrapped in white paper like snow, and we dance about the tree and sing songs to St. Nicholas."

"We sing too!" cried Anton. "And our tree is covered with little candles. It stands in the big guest room under the cuckoo clock. But our gifts are spread out on the kitchen table, with pine branches and holly on top of each."

"And I had a necklace made out of walnut shells," cried Trini. "Vaterli carved them like tiny edelweiss and strung them on a silk cord."

"Last Christmas I had a sled. Vaterli made it himself, and the blacksmith fastened on its metal runners," shouted Anton, for the wind was rising yet higher.

"And I had the pink coat and hood that I wore here from Bern. Mutterli sewed them herself," screamed Trini so that Anton could hear. She was skipping up and down, shivering no longer, with cheeks aglow with excitement.

"We had apples, and sweet chocolate filled with nuts, and cinnamon cake for supper," shouted Anton. "And they were all wrapped in silvered paper, and we did not know what we were choosing till we opened them."

"We had custard—"

"The goats!" exclaimed Anton, and he stopped to listen. *Tinkle, tinkle, tinkle* from among the rocks in the pasture land above came the soft jingling of bells.

Anton leaped ahead like a goat himself. Trini sprang after him like a young chamois. Yes, the goats were there! They were running merrily round among the rocks, poking their soft noses among the stones to nibble the sweet herbs that grew there. The little bells tied to the cords about their necks tinkled as though they were laughing at the two breathless children, for their long climb to the pasture.

Anton stood still a minute, blowing hard and beating his arms across his chest. Trini stamped her cold feet.

"*Alliho! Alliho!*" called Anton clearly. "*Hallo! Alliho!*"

The goats stopped eating and raised their heads to look at him.

"*Alliho! Alliho!*" Anton called again, and the three animals with an indignant bleat came slowly toward him. They seemed unhappy because their fine feast was taken from them. They came shaking their heads and bleating loudly.

Anton stroked each head and tapped each gently with his alpenstock. Then he started down the mountain

138

side, the goats following after. Trini danced along beside him.

Oh, how cold it was! The wind roared louder, and the tree tops swayed and bent. Very glad the children were to spy the tall chimney of the chalet. They were at home!

Soon the goats were nicely stabled in the cattle shed near the cheesery, while Anton and Trini were drinking warm milk and eating sweet brown bread before the fire in the kitchen.

GOODBYE, FATHER FLY EYES!

Trini was going home to Bern the next morning. It was Friday night, and the kitchen in the little chalet was buzzing with good cheer.

Sausage was sitting by the fire licking her fur. She was a grown-up cat now, plump and sleek from drinking so much rich cream. Trini sat near her, lining a basket in which Sausage was to make the journey back to Bern. The Traveler was already on her way to Greece, for Trini had opened the door of the cage and the swallow had flown joyously away.

Mother Fasel and Mother Rämi were busy packing boxes and bags and tucking into their corners the wool stockings that Trini had scarcely worn all summer.

Father Fasel and Father Rämi were out near the cattle shed cleaning the automobile to have it shining and ready for the long trip through the mountains to Bern.

And Regina Barrelet was to go back to her Hidden Valley. Father Fasel was to drive her to the nearest railroad station, and there she would take a train on her way to the Valley of Lötschen.

Anton and Trini were excited. Anton knelt near the stove, trying to strap the leather bag that held Trini's clothes.

"Here!" Trini called, running to Anton and holding out an old brass cowbell. "Here, you must pack this too.

140

Vaterli Rämi gave it to me when he bought the new one. I am going to hang this on my bedroom door at home, so that Mutterli will ring it to wake me in the morning."

Anton shook his head. The bag was full already. Besides all Trini's petticoats and dresses and shoes and aprons, there were the wooden shoes and many packages of flower seeds that she was to carry home to plant in the garden back of her house. They had all been crowded into the bag.

"It will not hold one thing more," said Anton decidedly. "Just wear the bell yourself!" He pushed the cover with his foot, but it refused to close.

"Why, Anton, people would think I was a cow!" giggled Trini.

"Well, be a cow! If you were, could not you stay all the year round at our chalet?" laughed Anton.

Trini jingled her bell a moment, then poked it into the bag.

"There! It is in! Shut the bag quickly," she cried. And sitting down on the bag, she snapped it shut. "Strap it, Anton! Strap it!"

"You think you are wise!" grumbled Anton. But he made haste and pulled the long straps together, and pressed down the brass latch into its hole.

"It is fastened!" he said.

Knock, knock, knock, at the kitchen door. It flew open, and in walked old Father Fly Eyes. He carried a red bundle.

"So the little Wise One is going away!" he exclaimed,

and after greeting the mothers, he stood by the warm stove holding the mysterious package.

"What have you there, Father Fly Eyes?" asked Anton, poking the red cloth tied about the bundle.

"Have you new children in that?" asked Trini. She came close to the old wood-carver and pulled the fringes that dangled from the edges of the cloth.

"These children of mine are just two days old," chuckled Father Fly Eyes.

He sat down on the lower step of the stove and placed the bundle on his knees.

"Just two days old!" he chuckled again.

"Show them!" the children begged.

Slowly Father Fly Eyes' fingers untied the string. Slowly he unwound the red cloth. Anton and Trini could scarcely wait while he folded back one corner, then another, till the bundle lay open on his lap.

It was a carved box, a lovely, long, slender box that Father Fly Eyes held high for them to see. It could hold pencils, erasers, and even bits of sweet chocolate. Trini's eyes danced and her fingers danced too, wanting to hold it.

And what a knife! It was a man's knife, a glistening sharp knife. It was lying on the cloth. Its wooden handle was handsomely carved. Anton drew in his breath when he saw it, with longing to have it for his own. He thought it was the finest knife anywhere about.

"There!" exclaimed Father Fly Eyes.

He dropped the lovely box into Trini's apron.

142

"This child," said he, "is for you to carry to Bern. It will hold all your pencils when you go to school near Lucerne."

Trini did not say a word. She could not. She looked down at the box of chestnut wood, then took it timidly in both hands to examine it. Then she cried out:

"Thank you! Thank you, dear Father Fly Eyes! You have carved your own little house here. I see it plainly. And here is the tall chimney and the fir tree growing by it. And there are the mountains afar off. You have carved them all here!"

She caught the old man's hands and rubbed them against her rosy cheeks, murmuring, "Thank you! Thank you!"

"Open it! Open it!" he smiled.

Trini lifted the carved cover. Inside lay a wooden bear, a nutcracker of a bear!

"Oo-oo-oo!" cried Trini. "I can put nuts in his mouth, and he will crack them!"

All this time Anton's eyes had been fixed on that knife. He thought it the best of Father Fly Eyes' children. It would certainly cut better than any other knife in the canton.

"Antonli," said the old man, suddenly turning to him, "if you are to be a wood-carver, you must have good tools. This is for you." And he held out to him, as he spoke, the precious knife.

"Oh!" Anton could scarcely believe that it was truly his. He examined the fine carvings on the handle. Tiny grape vines trailed over the wood, and on the top was perched a chamois with raised head and slender legs.

Carefully, with one finger, Anton felt the keen edge of the blade and whispered, "Kind Father Fly Eyes! I will carve handsome boxes with this, like the little box Joseph made in the Wooden Village."

That pleased Father Fly Eyes. He nodded, smiling, and looked deep into the folds of the cloth.

"There is still one more of my children here, one for the pretty teacher who lives in the Hidden Valley," and as he spoke he drew something from the wrappings and pointed to Regina.

"Regina! Come!" and Trini darted across the room to the long bench where Regina sat near sleeping Dete. Trini caught her arm and drew her over to the old woodcarver, who placed his gift in Regina's hands.

"How kind you are!" she exclaimed, surprised. "Look, Antonli! Look, Trini! It is a bottle to hold ink. It shall stand on my desk in the schoolroom for all the Lötschenthal children to see."

Trini and Anton gathered close and admired the daintily carved case, with the glass ink well in the center and tiny boys and girls dancing about the wooden sides.

At that moment Father Fasel entered the kitchen, and Father Rämi followed, holding a lantern. The automobile was cleaned and ready for the next day's journey.

Then there was noise and confusion in the kitchen. The men stood by the stove talking. Dete awoke and sat up. The mothers were laughing and bustling about. Anton and Trini were talking excitedly about their gifts, and Regina was smiling happily over her pretty ink bottle.

Then Father Rämi suddenly clapped his hands. Every one stood silent.

"We hope, God willing," said he, "to meet again in this chalet next summer. But before we part for a happy, busy winter, let us sing together a verse of the patriot song of our Switzerland."

145

"Yes, yes!" came from all parts of the room.

Then Father Rämi and Father Fasel began to sing in deep, rich voices; the mothers joined in; Father Fly Eyes chirped; Regina sang like a bird; and Anton and Trini piped high and low, while baby Dete clapped her hands:

> "O Mountains, strong and free,
>   Echo the song that we
>   Sing to Liberty!
>   On this patriot strand,
>   Beloved of Switzerland,
>   Her sons, in heart and hand,
>   Will cherished be!"

PRONUNCIATION AND EXPLANATION
OF WORDS IN THIS BOOK

Aare or **Aar** (*är*), a river which rises among the glaciers of Switzerland and flows north into the river Rhine

alp, a high mountain, or, as on page 86, a mountain pasture. The high mountain ranges of Switzerland are called the Alps.

al′ pen stock, a long, strong staff, pointed with iron, used in climbing mountains

alp′horn or **al′pen horn,** a long, curved, wooden horn, which the Swiss mountaineer sounds at sunset; also used at festivals

Alt′dorf (*ält′dôrf*), a town in Switzerland, where stands a famous statue of William Tell

a nem′ o ne, the delicately colored wind-flower

An ton′ li (*än tōn′ lĕ*), little Anton

av′a lanche, a great mass of snow and ice sliding down a mountain side and carrying trees, rocks, and everything before it

bag′pipe, a musical wind instrument consisting of a leather bag with pipes inserted. The musician blows on one pipe, presses the bag under his arm, fingers the stops of another pipe, and thus makes shrill music. Some bags have four pipes.

bar′ons, noblemen

Bern (*bairn*), the capital of Switzerland. *Bern* means " bear." The story runs that many bears were killed there the day the city was founded.

Ber nese′ (*bair nēs′*), belonging to Bern

bod′ice, a close-fitting outside waist, such as the milkmaids are wearing in the picture on page 88

Bri enz′ (*brĕ ĕnz′*), a town at the foot of the Bernese Alps, famous for its wood-carving

cache-cache (*kăsh-kăsh*), French for "Hide ! Hide ! " — the game of hide-and-seek

ca ca'o (*ka kā' ô*), a tropical tree which yields a fruit from which chocolate is made

can' ton, one of the states into which Switzerland is divided

cat' tle songs, songs sung by Swiss herdsmen when driving their cattle to and from pasture. *Ranz des vache*, the French-Swiss name for a cattle song, means "lowing of the cows."

Chail let' (*shĭ yā'*), a French-Swiss family name

chal et (*shă lā'* or *shăl'â*), a Swiss house

cham ois (*shăm'ĭ* or *shă mwä'*), a goat-antelope living wild in the high mountains of central and southern Europe. It can bound up and down the steep mountains and leap wide ravines.

cha teau' (*shă tō'*), a nobleman's house

chees'er y, the hut or factory where cheeses are made. Switzerland is famous for its cheese.

cre vasse' (*krĕ väs'*), a crack in a glacier, often very wide and deep

cuck'oo, a small brownish or grayish bird, said to lay its eggs in other birds' nests. German and Swiss wood-carvers make wooden clocks called "cuckoo clocks." A little door at the top of each clock snaps open on the hour, and a tiny wooden cuckoo pokes out its head and cries *cuckoo* at each stroke.

Czech (*chĕk*), a native of Bohemia, in central Europe

Det' e (*Dĕt'tē*), a Swiss name for a girl

eaves, the over-hanging edge of a roof

É cole' In ter na tion ale' (*ā kōl' ĕn̄ter nà'syō näl'*) International School at Geneva, for boys and girls

e'del weiss (*ā'dĕl vīs*), a small plant growing in the high Alps. The whole plant is thickly covered with short white hairs.

franc (*frănk*), a French coin, also in use in Switzerland

Franz'li (*fränz'le*), little Frank

Fri'bourg (*frē'bōōr*), the name of a canton in Switzerland, also the capital of this canton

Ge ne'va (*je nē'va*), a city on the lovely Lake of Geneva, in the canton of Geneva

gen'tian (*jĕn'shan*), a lovely, sky-blue flower

gla'cier (*glā'shẽr*), a slowly moving river of ice, formed in high mountain valleys

Gru yères' (*grü yair'*), a quaint old town in the canton of Fribourg, famous for its cheese

Gut'knecht (*gōōt'nĕkt*), a German-Swiss family name

Hay-Sunday Festival, a harvest festival. The Swiss celebrate the grape harvest also.

heath'cock, grouse. The Swiss grouse is something like our wild turkey.

Hel ve'tians (*hĕl vē'shanz*), the ancient name of the Swiss people. Their country was called Helvetia in olden times.

Jo hann'li (*Yō hän'lē*), little John, or Johnny

Ju'ra (*jōō'rȧ*), a mountain range between France and Switzerland

Lake of Ge ne' va, a beautiful, crescent-shaped lake, lying between Switzerland and France

la teen' sail, a triangular-shaped sail, as shown in the picture on page 106

Lau sanne' (*lō zȧn'*), the capital city of the Swiss canton of Vaud

Le Locle (*le lōkl*), a town in the canton of Neuchâtel, famous as the place where watch-making began in Switzerland, in the eighteenth century. Le Locle has now a watch-making institute and various industrial schools.

Lith u a'ni an, a native of Lithuania, a small country of Europe, west of Russia

Lot'schen Valley or **Lot'schen thal** (*lōōt'shĕn täl*), a quaint Swiss valley so surrounded by mountains and closed in by glaciers that it is almost cut off from the rest of the world. The people keep up many of their old customs and wear the old Swiss costume.

Lu cerne' (*lū surn'*), a canton of Switzerland; also the capital of this canton, on the Lake of Lucerne

Ma thilde' (*mȧ tēld'*), a woman's name

Mont Blanc' (*môɴ bläɴ'*), the highest peak of the Alps. Its beetling crags, great glaciers, deep snows, and mighty ice-cap make its ascent dangerous. *Mont Blanc* is French for " white mountain."

Mount Jo rat' (*zhō rä'*), a Swiss mountain overlooking Lausanne

Mut'ter li (*moo' tẽr le*), little mother, a German-Swiss word

Neu châ tel' (*nû shà tĕl'*), the capital city of the canton of Neu-châtel, by the Lake of Neuchâtel. Watches, jewelry, electrical apparatus, and cheeses are made at Neuchâtel.

peas'ant (*pĕz'ănt*), in Europe, a person of the lower class who lives in the country and works on a farm

quay (*kē*), a landing by the water, often very long; or a wharf, where ships dock

rho do den'drons (*rō dō dĕn'drons*), beautiful flowers, growing in clusters on large shrubs or trees, usually found in mountainous regions

Rhone (*rōn*), a river rising in south central Switzerland and flowing through Geneva and the Lake of Geneva, and on into France

rock-rose, a shrub with lovely flowers, looking like a dwarf rho-dodendron

Ro mansch' (*ro mănsh'*), a language spoken in a part of Switzerland

Ro'schen (*rō'shĕn*), German-Swiss for "little rose"

Rousseau' (*rōō sō'*), a famous French-Swiss writer and educator, born at Geneva, 1712

Rüt'li (*rōōt'le*), a meadow in the canton of Uri, called "the cradle of Swiss liberty." There, in 1307, a body of Swiss patriots swore to free their country from Austrian tyranny.

sap' phire (*săf' ĭr*), a precious stone of a beautiful blue color. Tiny sapphire jewels are used in watches.

St. Ber nard' Pass, a high mountain pass east of Mont Blanc. Almost at the summit of the pass, where it freezes even in sum-mer, dwell the monks of St. Bernard, who, with the aid of their famous dogs, used to rescue travelers lost in the snow. Nowa-days it is not necessary for travelers to go that way.

soap'stone, a stone soft enough to cut with a knife. It is used in many ways — for making stoves, foot-warmers, griddles, table tops, washtubs, and electric switchboards.

St. Gotth'ard Tun'nel (*gŏth'ard*), a mighty tunnel, cut through the massive mountain group of St. Gotthard in Switzerland. Trains running through this tunnel connect Genoa in Italy with Ger-many. In the old days, people had to travel by the carriage route over the top of the mountains.

St. Nich'o las (*nĭk'o las*), the popular Christmas saint of Europe, who is supposed to give presents like our Santa Claus. His day is December 6.

sun'set hour. In some parts of Europe at the sunset hour the church bells ring and everyone, in field or house, bows the head for a moment in prayer. The sunset hour in the Swiss Alps is made very lovely by the echoes of the alphorn.

Swiss cos'tumes. In the old days, each canton of Switzerland had its quaint costume. Today Switzerland is modern, and few of its people wear the old Swiss costume except on Sundays and holidays

Swiss fac'tor ies. In modern Swiss factories, run by electricity, are made cheeses, condensed milk, silk, ribbons, lace, cotton goods, milk chocolate, and other commodities. The Swiss rivers and waterfalls furnish a vast amount of electric power.

Swiss flag. The flag of Switzerland is red, with a white cross in the center. In 1863 people from various nations gathered at Geneva to make up a set of rules regarding the care of sick and wounded, which all countries should follow in time of war. The badge chosen by this conference for their work was the Swiss flag reversed in colors — a white flag with a red cross. So began the Red Cross societies.

Tri'ni (*Trē'ne*), a Swiss name for a girl

Up-the-Alp Day, the day on which cattle are driven into high mountain pastures to spend the summer. There the herdsmen or dairy maids live in huts, tend the cattle, and make butter and cheese.

U'ri (*ōō'rè*), a canton of Switzerland

Va'ter li (*fä'tĕr lĕ*), little father, a German-Swiss word

Vaud (*vō*), a canton of Switzerland

vil'lage herd. It is an Alpine custom for the people of a village to send their flocks and herds to pasture, all in care of the same herdboy or herdsman.

yo'del ing, the singing of the Swiss mountaineers

Zu'rich (*zōō'rĭk*), the largest city in Switzerland and the capital of the canton of Zurich. It stands on the shores of the beautiful Lake of Zurich, with the snow-crowned Alps in the background.

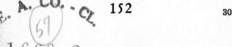